"Bodie can sleep on the ride back."

"Let me take her," Rex offered. "The brim of my hat will give her some shade."

Callie looked down at her sleepy baby. "All right."

He tightened the cinches on the saddles again while Callie fashioned a sling for her daughter. Bodie whimpered a mild protest as they slung her sideways against Rex's chest, her head nestled in the hollow of his shoulder, but then she reached up a little hand and laid it against his throat, as if feeling the beat of his pulse was all she needed to lull her to sleep.

Callie heard herself whisper, "She loves you."

"I love her, too," Rex said softly. He looked up then, his blue eyes as pale and warm as the summer sky. "I'll miss the two of you if you leave the ranch."

If, not *when*. Confused, Callie dared not reply to that. Anything she said would lay bare her heart, and that simply was not wise.

Arlene James has been publishing steadily for nearly four decades and is a charter member of RWA. She is married to an acclaimed artist, and together they have traveled extensively. After growing up in Oklahoma, Arlene lived thirty-four years in Texas and now abides in beautiful northwest Arkansas, near two of the world's three loveliest, smartest, most talented granddaughters. She is heavily involved in her family, church and community.

Books by Arlene James

Love Inspired

The Prodigal Ranch

The Rancher's Homecoming

Chatam House

Anna Meets Her Match
A Match Made in Texas
Baby Makes a Match
An Unlikely Match
Second Chance Match
Building a Perfect Match
His Ideal Match
The Bachelor Meets His Match
The Doctor's Perfect Match

Eden, OK

His Small-Town Girl
Her Small-Town Hero
Their Small-Town Love

Visit the Author Profile page at Harlequin.com for more titles.

The Rancher's Homecoming

Arlene James

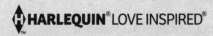

HARLEQUIN® LOVE INSPIRED®

Recycling programs
for this product may
not exist in your area.

LOVE INSPIRED BOOKS

ISBN-13: 978-0-373-81931-7

The Rancher's Homecoming

www.Harlequin.com

Printed in U.S.A.

But when you do a charitable deed,
do not let your left hand know what your
right hand is doing, that your charitable deed
may be in secret; and your Father who sees
in secret will Himself reward you openly.
—*Matthew* 6:3–4

In memory of my dad, William Fred "Bill" Roper, who taught me that country men are strong, resilient, capable, patient, accepting, funny, interesting, knowledgeable, talented, intelligent, clever, kind, neighborly and loving. I miss you.

Chapter One

Never let it be said that God did not answer prayers. Callie Deviner's answer walked into the War Bonnet Café on the morning of the last Thursday in May, ordered breakfast, which he wolfed down with three cups of black coffee, then calmly announced to all within hearing distance that he was looking for a live-in cook and housekeeper.

Callie set aside the heavy metal spatula she was holding and pushed a wisp of fine blond hair from her forehead with the back of her wrist before speaking to the freckle-faced teenager at the grill beside her.

"Fill this next order. I have to go out front."

The teen boy gaped at her. Johnny had been working at the café for more than six months and knew his way around a grill, but the regular cook, Chet, who was out with a toothache and as set in his ways as her father, still hadn't trusted the kid to do more than dish up fries and make toast. Callie ignored the youngster's sputtered assurances and moved toward the swinging metal door that separated the kitchen from the dining room, sweeping the hated net from her short hair as she did so.

Tucking the hairnet into the pocket of her apron with one hand and fluffing her bangs with the other, she moved swiftly behind the counter, past the middle-aged waitress, Jenny, and came to stand directly behind the tall, brown-haired man in the worn plaid shirt.

"Did I hear you say you were looking for a cook and housekeeper?"

His elbows slipped from the counter, and he spun on the stool to face her, his pale blue gaze quickly sweeping over her. He looked oddly polished despite that worn shirt. Without it, she'd have pegged him for a city boy, though she judged him to be in his thirties.

"That's right. For my father. We need someone live-in, as soon as possible. Dad's ill, and I've come to help out. My sisters will be along as soon as they can arrange it, but that could be several weeks, and until then, we've got to have help."

"Who is your dad?"

"Wes Billings."

"Oh. Out at Straight Arrow Ranch."

"That's right."

"I had heard that Wes was ill."

"Very ill, I'm afraid."

A murmur of condolence went around the room. Wes was well thought of around War Bonnet, Oklahoma. He was known to be a fair, honest, upright Christian man willing to help a neighbor in need. This had to be Rex Billings, Wes's son. He was quite a bit older than Callie, eight or ten years, so she didn't really know him. Even in a town as small as War Bonnet, that many years apart in school practically guaranteed they'd be strangers unless they both stayed in town, and to her knowledge Rex had never returned after leaving for college, except perhaps to visit.

He swept the room with his gaze, sending curious diners back to their own business. Callie inched closer, lowering her voice.

"I'll certainly do all I can for Wes. As for the position, how much are you thinking of paying?"

Rex quietly named a weekly figure that made Callie's heart leap with joy. Even two or three weeks at that rate would help her and her daughter, Bodie, get out of her father's house at last. She motioned to the empty plate on the counter in front of him.

"You might be interested in knowing that I cooked your breakfast. Two eggs over easy, bacon, very crisp, and flapjacks. Right? How'd I do?"

Billings grinned and parked both elbows on the counter again, one on either side of his plate. "Eggs were perfect. Flapjacks nearly floated off the plate. I like my bacon crisp to the edge of burnt, but that's just me. When can you start?"

"That depends," she said, sending up a silent prayer. "I have a six-month-old daughter. Will that be a problem?"

Rex Billings tilted his head. His thick, medium-brown hair, she noticed, had been expertly cut and styled. He wore it without a part and, even mussed, it looked adorable. Pretty much everything about him made a woman look twice, from his straight nose to his square jaw and chin. He had recently shaved; she could still smell the shaving cream. But already she could see the dark shadow of his beard beneath his evenly tanned skin. It was his eyes that did it, though. Pale blue and gem bright, as if backlit by tiny lightbulbs from within.

"Women with babies have been cooking and

cleaning for millennia," he said from behind a smile. "We have space for the both of you, especially if you don't mind sharing a room."

"Not at all."

"I can't imagine Dad would object. He knows you, doesn't he?"

"He does. He's known me my whole life." Callie reached around behind her and started untying her apron. "I can start right now, if you want."

"Works for me," he said, pushing up to his full height, which she judged to be at least a couple inches over six feet. His jeans, in contrast to his shirt, looked to be brand-new. "I suppose I ought to least get your name, though."

"Oh! I'm sorry!" Callie laughed, lifting the apron's neck piece off over her head. "It's Callie Deviner. Everyone just calls me Callie."

"Callie Deviner. Pleased to meet you." He put out his big hand. She quickly shook hands with him. "I'm Rex Billings."

"Yes, I figured that, since Wes has just the one son."

He tilted his head again, those pale blue eyes holding her gaze. "Shouldn't I know you, too?"

"I went to school with your sisters. You were long gone when I came on the scene."

"Ah. I suppose that's true. Meredith is ten years younger than me, so…"

"I'm Ann's age," Callie supplied. "Twenty-eight."

"Still, that's eight years," he said. "I was already practicing law by the time you graduated high school."

A lawyer. Wes must be very proud. She frowned then, wondering what ailed Wes. The sooner she got to the ranch, the sooner she'd know.

"Just let me get my things so we can go," she said.

He glanced around. "You sure it's all right to leave like this?"

"I'm just filling in. Off-the-books. It's fine."

"Okay, then." He nodded decisively, and she carried her apron toward Jenny.

The blocky, chatty waitress looked around in surprise when Callie thrust the thick, white apron into her hands, saying, "I'm leaving now, Jenny."

"Leaving?" Jenny echoed. "Who's gonna cook?"

"Johnny can handle it."

"But—"

"I don't actually work here," Callie reminded the woman, who followed her into the back room. "I'm not even being paid. It isn't as if you can fire me. I'm just helping out."

"Your daddy—"

"Will get over it," Callie said softly. Or not. Either way, she was going with Rex Billings. "You let me worry about that."

"Chet will be beside himself," Jenny hissed.

Callie ignored her, taking her handbag from the locked cabinet and tossing Jenny the key. "I won't be needing this again."

One more thing she wouldn't need to do again was put up with Ben Dolent and her father's heavy-handed matchmaking. Ben wasn't a bad man, just a dull, unattractive one who happened to be the manager of her father's grain silo, a willing pawn of her father's, doing whatever he was told without question. Sometimes Callie thought that if she had to endure one more evening of his company she would explode.

"Stuart is not going to be happy about this," Jenny warned, but Callie couldn't remember when her father had last been happy about anything, especially not where she was concerned. She knew he meant well, but financial security was not the only important thing in life, and her father had no right to decide whom she would marry and where she would live. Still, no matter how hard she tried, she couldn't seem to make him understand that. The more she talked, the more he restricted her access to funds and threw Ben Dolent at her.

"Do me a favor, Jenny," she said softly. "Don't call my father yet."

"I have to, girl! He owns this place."

"Just give me a couple hours then. That's not too much to ask, is it? How often have I helped you out?"

Jenny's lips, red with her favorite lipstick, flattened, but then she nodded, muttering, "It's about to get real busy around here." She glared at Callie. "You couldn't have picked a worse time to up and leave. I don't know where all these folks are coming from. It's a phenomenal, is what it is, a phenomenal."

"Phenomenon," Callie corrected gently. Smiling, she patted Jenny's arm as she left the small room. "Thanks, Jenny. I appreciate it."

Callie walked out into the dining room, the strap of her roomy handbag slung over one shoulder, and smiled at Rex Billings, the tall, handsome lawyer.

"I'm all yours."

The way his pale blue gaze raked over her, from the top of her shaggy blond head to the toes of her cheap athletic shoes, suddenly made her wish that she'd phrased that differently, but then he smiled and lifted an arm in invitation.

"After you."

It didn't hit Rex until she pointed to the tall, redbrick house in the center of the block exactly whom he had hired.

"You're Stuart Crowsen's daughter."

She turned wide, glade-green eyes on him, seeming almost frightened. "Is that a problem?"

"Of course not. I just didn't realize, that's all."

"Because of my married name," she concluded, nodding.

He turned the six-year-old pickup truck into the drive and brought it to a stop. His own silver, two-seater sports car sat under a protective cloth cover beneath a tree behind his dad's house. "I take it you're divorced."

"No." The sadness in that one word said it all.

"I'm sorry," he told her, killing the engine and letting out the clutch. "Divorced is no picnic, but widowed has to be worse."

"You're divorced, then?"

"Yeah." He sighed and rubbed a finger over his eyebrow. "No kids, so at least we didn't mess up innocent lives."

It turned out that catching the boss's daughter cheating on him had an upside, even if she was your own wife. Rex had ended his relationship with his former law firm, not to mention his marriage with the senior partner's daughter, over eight months ago. Given the situation, Rex had been offered a very generous severance package. That had given him the freedom to come back to War Bonnet and help out with the ranch while his dad fought to recover his health.

"I'd just found out I was pregnant when Bo died," Callie told Rex softly. "Bodie will never know him, and he never saw her, but I thank God that I have her."

"Sounds like you've had a rough time of it."

"Mmm, well, no one's sick. Mind if I ask what's wrong with your dad?"

"Cancer. They removed a piece of his liver and some lymph glands, but at least it wasn't in his pancreas or bile ducts. He'll have to undergo chemotherapy when he's stronger, which is why my sisters and I are coming home for a while. This is a busy season at the ranch, and he just can't manage on his own. With Mom gone, it's up to us."

"I remember when your mom died," Callie said. "It was a big shock. I don't think anyone realized she had a heart condition."

"No one," Rex confirmed. "It was a birth defect. All us kids had to be tested for it afterward. Thankfully, none of us have the problem, but I think that's why Meredith became a nurse."

"I wondered about that. Meri never said anything about wanting to be a nurse when we were girls."

"I didn't know you were that close."

"We hung out some."

Callie reached for the door handle. "I'll be as quick as I can. There's a portable crib in the garage. Also some boxes and tape. I used them when Bodie and I moved in a few months back. If you want to help out, you can put the crib in the truck while I tape up the boxes. Then we'll go inside."

"That'll work."

They walked into the garage via a side door. Callie pulled out the crib and Rex carried it out to the truck. When he returned to the garage, she had four midsize moving boxes put together. She handed him two and took two in her hands before leading the way through the side door.

"Most of my clothes are on hangers," she said, stepping up into a pristine kitchen. "Bodie's things will fit in two boxes."

"You been keeping house for your dad?" he asked, glancing around.

"Almost my whole life," she confirmed. He nodded to himself. Okay, she could cook *and* clean. "Don't worry," she added. "He can afford to hire help."

That worked for Rex. "Just take what you need for now. We can come back later for anything else."

She turned and faced him. "I'd rather take it all if you don't mind. There really isn't that much." Nervously, she sifted her fingers through her short, silky bangs.

He'd always preferred women with long hair, but Callie's wispy, chin-length blond hair suited her oval face. He liked her somewhat pointy chin. It looked good on her, as did the form-hugging jeans and the simple, short-sleeved T-shirt that she wore. She looked strong and fit, curving in all the right places. Everything about her felt completely genuine.

Rex realized that he was staring and, to cover his lapse, blurted out, "What color is that shirt?"

She looked down at her shirt. "What?"

"I can't figure out if it's orange or pink," he said with a chuckle.

Her green eyes—the color of leafy trees sparkling in the sunlight—rolled upward, and pink lips without a trace of lipstick widened in a smile. "It's *melon*."

He grinned. "Whatever you say."

Smiling, she crooked a finger at him. "Come with me."

"Lead on."

They walked through a formal dining room and into an entry hall, where a staircase led up to the second floor. A plump, grandmotherly woman with tightly curled, iron gray hair appeared on the landing above them.

"Callie? Shouldn't you be at the café?"

"Not today, Mrs. Lightner. Has Bodie had her bottle?"

"She has, as well as a bath and a fresh diaper. I was just about to dress her when I heard you come in."

"That's wonderful. You're a blessing, Mrs. Lightner. Would you finish dressing her for me?"

The elderly woman frowned, her brows meeting behind her large, thick glasses. Rex figured he knew what the problem must be. He set down the boxes.

"Are you the Mrs. Lightner who used to teach me in Sunday school and give my sisters Meredith and Ann piano lessons?"

Those eyebrows went up. "Meredith and Ann? You must be Rex Billings."

"That's right." Smiling, he stepped up onto the landing and hugged the woman. "I wasn't sure at first, ma'am. I thought you were older."

Tittering and fluffing her hair, she actually blushed. "Really?"

"You know how it is," he said, grinning at her. "Kids think anyone over twenty is ancient. You couldn't have been much older than thirty back then." She'd been fifty if she'd been a day, but he'd learned to schmooze at the best law firm in Tulsa.

"Oh, go on," Mrs. Lightner said with a giggle. "You always were a scamp."

"I suppose I was," he admitted good-naturedly. "I'm glad to see you, though. I'll be sure to tell Dad."

She sobered then. "How is Wes? I heard he wasn't doing too well."

Rex nodded. "It's been tough. The surgery was hard on him, but my sisters and I are going to take good care of him."

"You tell him I'm praying for him."

"Yes, ma'am. We appreciate that."

"I'll be in to take over in a just a moment, Mrs. Lightner," Callie said. Then she crooked her finger at Rex again. "This way."

Mrs. Lightner still frowned, but she went off to dress Bodie while Rex picked up the boxes and followed Callie into another room.

The place had a faded, girlish feel about it. Callie wasted no time packing her belongings quickly and efficiently. Within minutes, Rex began carting boxes and bundles of clothing down to the truck. He returned to find Mrs. Lightner standing in the doorway, the baby in her arms and a thunderous expression on her face.

"What on earth is going on here?"

"Didn't I say?" Callie replied smoothly, never slowing her movements. "Mr. Billings needs my help until his daughters arrive."

Sensing a battle on the horizon, Rex quickly surveyed the field and decided on a course of action. Sliding past Mrs. Lightner, he took a quick glance at the baby and carried the suitcases that Callie had packed downstairs. He heard the argument erupt behind him.

"You can't do that!"

"But I must, Mrs. Lightner. Wes Billings desperately needs help."

Rex didn't linger to hear more. The sooner he got Callie Deviner out of there and to the ranch, the better for all concerned. He returned to find Callie in the nursery tossing baby things into a box while Mrs. Lightner rocked a babbling pink bundle who seemed determined to snatch glasses from teary eyes.

"I'm sure you know what you're doing,"

Mrs. Lightner said in a tone that clearly indicated the very opposite.

"We'll be fine," Callie promised, closing the box. "Thank you for your concern." She glanced up at Rex then, sliding the box across the carpet toward him. "We really have to go."

"Yes, I don't want to leave Dad any longer than I must," he stated honestly. "One of the ladies from church is sitting with him, but she has to leave soon."

Callie slid another box toward him, then shouldered an overstuffed diaper bag and stood, turning to the rocking chair. Mrs. Lightner sighed as Callie gathered the baby into her arms. Dipping, Callie snagged the top of a large plastic bag of disposable diapers.

Rex stacked and picked up the boxes. They felt surprisingly light, so he took the diapers from Callie.

"If you've got all that," she said, "I can grab the car seat from the closet downstairs."

"What about the rest of these things?" he asked, nodding at the elaborate stroller and the padded playpen, the changing table and canopied baby bed.

"Leave them," Callie instructed briskly.

He didn't have to be told twice. "Okay, then. Let's move."

Within minutes they were packed into the

truck, and Callie was hugging Mrs. Lightner in the driveway.

"Go on home now, Mrs. Lightner," he heard her say, "and thanks again for everything."

"But your father…" Mrs. Lightner said.

"Don't worry. Just head on home."

As they backed out of the driveway, Rex couldn't help asking, "Everything okay?"

Callie smiled and glanced over her shoulder at the baby before settling into her seat with a satisfied sigh. "It is now."

Rex wondered why she seemed so anxious to take this job, but he was too glad of the help to care. The sooner his dad was on the mend, the sooner he could get back to his real life. The sooner *everyone* could get back to their real lives, him, his sisters, their dad, even Callie Deviner.

Hiring the daughter of the wealthiest man in War Bonnet as a cook and housekeeper did seem odd, but Rex didn't really care what the pretty little widow's reasons were for taking this job. He had to give her this: she was a decisive woman, and she traveled light and fast.

He could've done worse. Casually looking over at her, he smiled.

Oh, yes. He could have done much worse.

Chapter Two

Wes greeted Callie and her little daughter, Bodie, with the brightest smile Rex had seen in weeks.

"I'm tickled pink to be here," Callie told him. "You just don't know. Now, I'm going to get the baby down for a nap, clean that kitchen floor and start on your lunch."

"Ah, I don't have much appetite," Wes said, picking at the coverlet on his bed.

"Listen, you," Callie threatened teasingly, "I have your wife's recipe for pimento cheese, and I'm not afraid to use it. I'm counting on there still being jars of the pimentos she put up in the pantry."

Wes's eyes filled with tears as he beamed. "I never knew what to do with them."

"Need any help getting dressed and to the table?" she asked, patting Wes on the shoulder.

Rex knew his father hadn't been out of his pajamas since he'd come home from the hospital.

Rex could've kissed Callie then and there.

Wes shook his head and rasped, "I'll manage."

"I'll help him before I go out and get to work on the baler again. The girls stocked up on groceries before they left, so I think you'll find everything you need in the kitchen. If not, let me know. I'll send someone back into town."

Nodding, Callie left to settle the baby and get started on her work, the little one riding her hip. Rex helped Wes dress in loose jeans and a soft T-shirt. Wes even combed his thick, sugar-and-cinnamon hair, complaining about the heavy graying at his temples and needing a trim.

"We'll get you to the barber as soon as you're back on your feet," Rex promised. Then he went out to tackle that old baler again.

The Straight Arrow Ranch still baled the old small, rectangular bales and stored them in pole barns situated strategically around the property because only about 25 percent of its two square miles of land was suitable for growing fodder, and much of the range to the north and west was too rough for transporting the large, round bales to which so many ranchers had gone. Besides, they already had the storage facilities, so it didn't make sense to fix what wasn't broken, as Wes put it. Except that the hay baler was currently broken, and Rex wasn't making much headway fixing it.

Wes sat at the kitchen table when Rex came in for lunch, exasperated and determined not to show it. Story of his life lately. He saw no sign of the wheelchair that he'd rented, probably because Wes hated to use it, but Rex didn't care how his dad had gotten to the table as long as he was there. He sent Callie a smile of thanks as he walked to the counter and helped himself to a tall glass of iced tea.

"How did you know he loved Mom's pimento cheese sandwiches?" he asked softly.

She gave him the barest of smiles, whispering, "I've seen him eat three at a sitting."

Saluting her with his tea glass, Rex walked to the table. He silently congratulated himself on making a good hire.

Church ladies had been helping them out since Rex's sisters had left after getting Wes home from the hospital, providing casseroles and other dishes and sitting with Wes when called upon, but it had rapidly become obvious that they couldn't continue to impose. The past couple weeks on their own had been rough, especially with the ranch taking more and more of Rex's time. Rex honestly hadn't expected to find someone to help so quickly, though. He'd only stopped at the café because he was hungry for a decent breakfast. Even before his sisters had returned to their respective jobs—Ann to Dallas, where she managed a hotel, and Meredith to Oklahoma City, where she worked as a nurse in the hospital where their father had been through surgery and would soon start chemotherapy—breakfast had been an issue. Even a well-stocked larder didn't help if a person had no idea what to do with its contents.

Callie knew exactly what she was doing. Neither of his sisters could hold a candle to her in the kitchen. Even his mother might have had her work cut out for her. Gloria Billings had been fun, loving and more than a little scatterbrained. Callie proved efficient, quick and affable, not to mention easy on the eyes. Wes certainly seemed happy with what was on his plate, and Rex hadn't seen that in many months, even before they'd figured out what was wrong with his dad.

Eventually Wes wiped his mouth with a napkin, saying, "Wish I could do better by this, Callie. Sure is good. Any chance you can put it up for my lunch tomorrow?"

Callie turned from the big, old stove that had been Rex's mother's pride and joy. Gloria had loved everything about the rustic, sprawling, sixty-year-old cedar-sided ranch house, wrapped in deep porches and steep, metal roofing that Rex's grandfather had built. She'd even loved the drafty, smoky, fieldstone fireplace that took up one whole wall in the L-shaped living and formal dining area. Smiling, Callie walked to the rectangular kitchen table and picked up Wes's plate.

"I think there's enough left over for your lunch tomorrow, if that's what you want. I was planning on Gloria's chicken and dumplings for supper."

Wes sat back with a happy smile. "It's been an age since I last had that."

"Gloria was generous with her recipes," Callie said. "I use them all the time."

As she carried the plate back to the sink, Wes looked to Rex. "You did good, son."

Rex just smiled and gobbled down the last of his thick sandwich, as a thin wail rose from upstairs.

Callie calmly moved toward the back stairs. A back hallway provided access to the stairs, a laundry room, mudroom, a small bath and what his mother had used to call her craft room. His dad had taken over the latter as his bedroom to spare himself a trip up the stairs after he'd taken ill. What had once been six small bedrooms upstairs had been remodeled into four bedrooms and two roomy baths, all with sloping ceilings.

"If you need me, I'll be in the barn," Rex announced as Callie climbed the stairs.

"Okay," Callie called. "We'll be fine."

"That baler still giving you trouble?" Wes asked with a shake of his head. "Wish I was up to helping you fix it."

"It's okay, Dad." Rex got to his feet. "Let's get you back to your room."

His father sighed but laboriously pushed into a standing position. At sixty-two years of age and six foot four inches in height, Wes still stood a couple inches taller than Rex, but he felt perilously thin when Rex wrapped his arm lightly about Wes's waist.

He walked his dad down the hall into his bedroom, which now contained a rented hospital bed. His sisters had draped a sheer curtain over the window, but Wes preferred to keep that pushed to one side. Rex thought it was so his father could see his mother's peonies. Even now, four years after her unexpected death, they bloomed in the shade of the old hackberry tree at the side of the house, though the flowerbeds badly needed weeding.

Rex made a mental note to see to the flowerbeds—just as soon as he got the baler operating and the early hay harvest under way. He had to get the hay in or the cattle wouldn't have the fodder they'd need to get through winter. The Straight Arrow covered 1,280 acres of prime ranchland, and a good portion of it had been sowed in sturdy grasses, but after several years of drought, even the good rains of the past year hadn't allowed the range to fully recover. With Dad's medical bills piling up—the insurance carried high deductibles and co-pays—the ranch couldn't afford to buy more fodder than usual and still stay on a sound financial footing, which was why Rex would be paying Callie's wages, though he intended for neither her nor his father to realize that fact. After all, he could afford it. Besides, he'd be practicing law again soon enough.

Ranching had never been Rex's chosen career path, but without the ranch, Rex and his sisters feared that their dad would simply give up. He'd taken their mother's death hard, and they feared that his cancer would become an excuse for him simply to let go and join her in the next life, especially if the ranch faltered. Rex couldn't let that happen. Though not as prosperous as in years past, the ranch remained on solid fiscal footing, and Rex intended to see to it that it stayed that way. As much as he disliked the physical labor of ranching, he could, *would*, do this.

Besides, Callie wouldn't be here for long. They'd only need her until Meredith could get a leave of absence from her nursing job and Ann's company sent a temporary manager to take over for her so she could use some of those many vacation days she had stacked up. Anyway, it was worth double Callie's wages to see Wes smiling, dressed and sitting at the table for meals again.

Meanwhile, having a pretty woman around the house, good meals on the table and clean clothes would go a long way toward helping Rex swallow his frustration and dismay with the work and do this thing for his dad. It was the least he could do for the man who had never pushed him to give up his own dreams to take over the family legacy.

After changing her daughter's diaper, Callie nursed her in the rocking chair in front of the empty fireplace. She watched through the window as Rex walked across the yard, past an enormous bur oak, over the hard-packed red dirt road to the big red barn on the other side. The old barn sagged a bit, its white roof beaten to gray in places by the Oklahoma weather, but it still stood proudly beside a maze of corrals and a conglomeration of newer metal outbuildings.

Rex pulled on a pair of leather work gloves as he walked, his big, booted feet kicking up little dust clouds along the well-worn path. She respected him for taking time out of his law practice to come here and care for his ailing father, but she had to wonder just how much he knew about balers and livestock.

Wes obviously needed the help. His gauntness had shocked Callie more than the sudden graying of his hair, and in order to tempt his appetite she'd instantly started sorting through her mental store of Gloria Billings's recipes and what she recalled the Billings girls had bought in her father's grocery.

Gloria had always been very kind to Callie and widely generous with her recipes. As a motherless girl who had always known she was a disappointment to her father—Stuart Crowsen obviously would have much preferred a son to take over his many businesses—Callie had deeply admired Gloria and envied Ann and Meredith.

She barely remembered Rex. He'd been away at college by the time she'd started to take notice of boys. She hadn't given the largely absent Rex a passing thought. She couldn't help doing so now, though.

He was a fine-looking man, and he so obviously loved his father.

"Thank You, Lord," she whispered, cradling Bodie against her. "Thank You for sending him into the café this morning. Thank You for this chance. Thank You for giving me a way to help Wes. Please show me how to make the most of it. I hope Gloria knows that I'll do my best by him."

Bodie pulled away and sat up then, giving Callie a milky smile. Callie hugged her, feeling for the first time since her husband, Bo, had died that they were truly going to be okay.

"We're on our way now, baby girl. Soon we'll be on our own."

The money that she would earn here with the Billings family would take her and Bodie to a new life, someplace where Callie could find a decent-paying job and make a home for the two of them. Far away from her father. Meanwhile, she would do her best to get Wes Billings back on his feet and Straight Arrow Ranch running smoothly.

She carried Bodie downstairs, created a playpen out of kitchen chairs, filled it with her daughter's favorite toys and went to work. This kitchen wasn't as modern as her father's. Even the microwave and dishwasher were ancient. The room had lots of space, though, and Callie loved the butcher-block work island.

Within the hour, the house was filled with the mouthwatering aroma of chocolate chip-and-walnut cookies. Wes called from his room, "Smells good!"

"I'll bring you a plate with a glass of milk."

She piled half a dozen cookies on a plate, poured a talk glass of whole milk and carried them to him, along with a stack of napkins.

"I can't eat all that," he protested.

"Eat what you want," she replied, leaving the snack on the bedside table within easy reach.

He helped himself to the first cookie, took a bite and closed his eyes, humming approval.

"Girl, you know your way around a kitchen."

"I had to learn early."

"I imagine you did."

"Gloria was a big help."

"My Glory was a jewel," he said on a sigh.

"I missed her after y'all switched your membership to Countryside Church."

"The pastor out there was the son of a good friend of mine," Wes explained, reaching for another cookie. "We wanted to support him. He's been gone awhile now, but by then we'd sunk pretty deep roots in that church. It's home."

"I understand," Callie said. "I've been thinking about going there myself."

Wes nodded and finished off the second cookie, then reached for the milk, saying, "You'll like it. Rex is gonna like these. That old baler is giving him a real hard time. Why don't you take him some?"

"I'll do that," Callie said.

Wes brightened appreciably. Callie smiled and returned to the kitchen, where she found a sturdy paper plate and a disposable cup. She filled the plate with cookies and the cup with milk. After parking Bodie on her hip, she went out through the front door, carrying the plate with the cup nestled in its center.

She entered the barn through the wide rolling door nearest the road. Rex was bent over the long, mechanical arm of the baler, growling at something.

"Maybe this will help," she said.

He jerked upright in surprise, a ratchet in his hand. His eyebrows peaked when he saw the plate of cookies and cup of milk. "Oh. Uh. Thanks."

"Your dad thought you might like a snack."

"Yeah. Looks good. Won't get that stupid bolt off, though," he grumped, laying aside the ratchet and stripping off his gloves.

She passed him the plate. He picked up a cookie and tasted it. "Mmm. Make these from scratch?"

"Of course."

"Dad eat any?"

"He did."

Rex smiled and winked. "Smart girl."

"He obviously needs to put on some weight," she noted.

"You've already gotten him to eat more than we've been able to since he came home from the hospital. You are a great find."

"Hold that thought," she chortled as he gobbled three cookies and chugged half the milk before handing her back the plate and picking up the ratchet again. She figured that she had a small window to make a good impression before her father made his displeasure known.

"Maybe I can get in there without my gloves," Rex mused, studying the baler.

"Why don't you lift the arm?" she asked.

"I tried that. More room from the top. Not that it matters. I still can't get in there to loosen the bolt so I can replace this part." He tapped an electrical receiver on the arm.

She set the plate on the fender of the baler and held out her hand. "Trade you. Give me the ratchet and hold Bodie."

"Uh…" He looked at the baby as if he'd never seen one before, and Callie hid a smile.

"She doesn't bite. Well, she does actually. She's teething. Just keep anything you don't want chomped on out of her mouth." Holding Bodie out with both hands, Callie waited for Rex to take her. He laid down the ratchet, reached, pulled back and gingerly reached out again. His enormous hands more than spanned Bodie's little torso. "Just tuck her into the fold of your arm," Callie instructed.

He seemed confused for a moment, but then he folded his left arm beneath the baby and pulled her against his chest. Bodie stuck her hand in her mouth and looked up at him, drooling. Callie picked up the ratchet and went to work.

"She's got your eyes," Rex said after a moment.

"Yep, and my hair, poor thing." Callie tilted her shoulder, maneuvering around the curved teeth of the baling arm.

"What's wrong with your hair?"

Callie almost had to lay her cheek on the arm of the baler to reach the bolt. "Fine, stick straight, can't make up its mind what color it is…"

"It's blond," he said, sounding confused.

"Several shades of blond." She found the bolt head and slotted the socket over it, but she couldn't get enough leverage to budge the thing. Straightening, she said, "We're going to need an adapter."

Rex walked over to the workbench against the wall and picked through the toolbox there, returning with a six-inch adapter, Bodie still tucked into the curve of his arm. She seemed perfectly comfortable there, one leg crossed over the other, her gaze studying him. Her pink ruffled booties and matching shorts were absolutely adorable, but Callie noticed that the T-shirt looked a little tight. After he handed over the adapter, he picked up another cookie from the plate on the fender. Callie fixed the socket to the adapter and the adapter to the ratchet.

"So you didn't go to the hair salon to get your hair like that?" he asked conversationally.

Sputtering laughter, Callie shook her head. "I've seen the inside of a hair salon exactly twice in my life. The second time was to fix what I had done the first time. Me and perms do not go together."

"Perms? Like curly hair?"

"Think corkscrews coming out of long, blond steel wool. I might as well have put my head in a fryer. I cut it off and I kept cutting it until the last of the damage was gone." She blew at her bangs. They tended to lie flat on her forehead. "It darkened up and got all stripy while I was pregnant with Bodie." She shrugged. "Nothing I can do about it."

"Why would you?" he asked. "I know women who pay small fortunes to have hair like that. It looks good."

She blinked at him, ridiculously pleased. "Thanks." Unable to remember the last time anyone had told her anything about her looked good, she focused on the job at hand, a little breathless.

Within moments, she had the socket firmly affixed to the bolt again, but she still couldn't budge it.

"You'll have to manage this," she said, turning her head to find Rex sharing his cookie with Bodie. "What are you *doing*? She can't eat that!" The little scamp smacked her lips in delight, her pale eyebrows arched high.

"I—I thought…I mean, I didn't know… She likes it," he finished lamely.

"Of course she *likes* it," Callie said, trying not to laugh, "but she's not supposed to *have* it." She pinned him with a direct look over her shoulder, her hands filled with the ratchet and bolt. "She's just started eating solid foods, and sugar, chocolate and nuts are *not* on the menu." Seeking to make a liar of her, Bodie leaned forward, her mouth nibbling on the bit of cookie that Rex still held in his fingers. "Will you please get rid of that and come here?" Callie barked.

He flung the cookie bit away and stepped toward her, wiping his hand on his shirt.

"You've got it on?" he asked in an incredulous tone.

"Yes. Now turn the thing."

He covered her hand with his much larger one and gave the ratchet a single Herculean wrench, then another and another... Callie felt the bolt drop into the socket cup.

"That's it. Short bolt."

Rex gave a huge sigh of relief and let go, backing away. "Woman, you are worth your weight in gold. I have been working on that for hours and hours."

Laughing, Callie carefully extricated the tool and the bolt from the machinery. "Replace your part, and I'll help you bolt it back on," she volunteered. "Might want to disconnect the battery first."

"Already done," he said, passing Bodie back to her. He smiled, and the warmth of it did funny things to Callie's insides. "Thank you," he went on. "Seriously. I couldn't have done this without you. And I'm sorry about the cookie," he added sheepishly.

"No problem." She handed over the ratchet but kept the bolt, pretending to study it, her heart beating a little faster than it should have.

He took her hand in his, studying the bolt

with her. The man's hand felt unusually warm, almost hot. Maybe that was why she shivered.

"This is rusty. No wonder it was so hard to get off," he said.

Realizing he was right, she cleared her throat. "Got any cleaner?"

"There's a jar with other bolts on the work-bench."

Pulling away from him, she carried the bolt to the workbench and added it to the jar of red-dish liquid before turning toward the house, Bodie riding her hip. "I'll go check on Wes, get the laundry started and come back."

"Great," Rex said. "Hey, how do you know so much about this stuff?"

She turned in midstride. "My dad owns the Feed and Grain, remember? And he didn't seem to know I was female until Teddy Gilmer asked me to the homecoming dance. Until then I was just after-school help with small hands that could get into tight places." She wiggled her fingers.

"Remind me to thank your dad," Rex said, smiling again and bowing slightly.

"Oh, I think you'll get your chance," Callie replied. Unfortunately, she doubted that any of the Billings family would feel any-thing close to gratitude once Stuart Crowsen showed himself.

She just hoped that she hadn't brought them more trouble. If anyone could stand up to Stuart Crowsen, though, it was Wes Billings.

At least, Wes could do it if he was physically stronger. She'd just have to pray that was the case, and in the meantime, she'd do all that she could to prove her worth around here—and keep her daughter from eating cookies.

Chapter Three

The afternoon turned hot, with temperatures shooting up to the midnineties. Surrounded by large trees and deep porches, the old house felt comfortable enough, except for the kitchen. Used to the central air-conditioning of her father's house, Callie soon felt herself flagging. She opened several windows, especially upstairs, and turned on all the ceiling fans she could find, including the one in the kitchen. Soon, a pleasant breeze cooled the place. She wondered how well that would do in the coming triple-digit heat of deep summer, however.

Figuring that Rex would need something cold, she made a pitcher of iced tea, then carried a glass to Wes, only to find him fast asleep. Pleased to see that he'd eaten all of his cookies and emptied his milk glass, she tiptoed away again, moved the laundry from the washer to the dryer and went out to help Rex reattach that bolt.

He drained the tumbler of iced tea that she brought him in one long gulp.

"You are quickly making yourself indispensable around here," he gasped, holding the cold glass against his forehead.

She just smiled. "I made the tea sweet because Wes can use the calories, but if you prefer it unsweetened, I can do that, too."

"I don't need the calories," he said, "but then I don't usually work like this. Either way is fine." He set aside the glass. "Did the AC unit kick on?"

"I didn't know there was an AC unit."

Rex sighed. "I think it's broken. Dad works outside so much, I doubt he's even bothered with it in years. For him, just getting out of the sun is usually enough. I'll take a look at it first chance I get."

Callie nodded, aware that Rex was overwhelmed at the moment. "Ready to replace that bolt?"

"Yep." He looked at Bodie, who rubbed her eyes with a fist. "Must be nap time."

"She doesn't get a nap until her momma's ready to start dinner," Callie said, jiggling the baby on her hip. "Let's do this. I've got clothes in the dryer."

"Everything's ready for you." He nodded at the tool and clean bolt waiting on the fender of the baler. "You've got the housework down to a science, don't you?" he muttered, gingerly taking Bodie into his hands.

"You'd be surprised how quickly you figure it out," Callie said, fitting the bolt head into the socket. "A few sleepless nights and haphazard days and it all starts falling into place. I trust you've tested the connections and everything works."

"Yes. Praise God! I'm serious. I have prayed repeatedly about this thing. I can't tell you how relieved I am to have it running. As it is, we have to use a custom cutter on the oats and sorghum. I was beginning to fear we'd have to hire someone to do the hay, too."

"Are you using Dean Paul Pryor for your custom cutting?" Callie asked, bending over the baler arm to find the bolt hole.

"I think that's who Dad mentioned. Do you know him?"

"Everyone knows Dean. When he sold his granddaddy's farm to pay for his equipment, everyone thought he was crazy. Well, my father did. Dad would have loaned him the money, but Dean didn't want to borrow. He said that way he stood to lose the farm and the equipment, and you know what? He was right." She finally found the hole and got the bolt seated. With a few quick turns, she had it secured. She looked over her shoulder at Rex, who was tapping Bodie's nose. "You'd better finish this."

"Ah." He came forward, wrapped his hand around hers on the ratchet and pulled.

She slipped her hand free, disturbed by the heat that radiated up her arm, and took Bodie from him. He grunted as he pulled the bolt tight.

"That should do it." Grinning, he shook the ratchet free and extricated it from the baler teeth. "You've earned your week's wages already."

Callie smiled, but then the sound of tires on the dirt road out front had them both looking in that direction. A moment later, a vehicle door slammed, and a male voice boomed, "Callie Dianne!"

Her heart beginning to pound, Callie swallowed and frowned apologetically at Rex. "I'm sorry about this," she said, aware that her voice trembled. "My father's come to call." She'd hoped to have more time. Reluctantly, she moved toward the front of the barn, silently praying that this confrontation wouldn't be as difficult as she feared.

She heard Rex set aside the tool and follow

her. Stuart had made it halfway up the path toward the house when Callie reluctantly called out to him.

"I'm here, Dad."

He spun around, a raging bull of a man. Not quite six feet tall and built like a brick wall, Stuart hadn't changed much in the past twenty years, but then he'd always seemed middle-aged, angry and overbearing. His flattop haircut added to the squareness of his face, as did his blunt nose and pugnacious chin. Callie had never been able to see anything of herself in him. Long ago, she'd learned to remain calm in the face of his rages, and he'd never physically hurt her, but he wielded power with purpose and impunity to achieve his own ends.

"Get in the car!" he demanded, pointing.

Callie took a deep breath, cradled Bodie against her, ignored the quaking of her own knees and shook her head. "No."

"You're going home."

Callie swallowed to steady her voice and said, "Wes needs me, Dad. I'm going to stay here to help Mr. Billings."

"Get in the car!" Stuart roared, starting toward her.

Despite the slamming of her heart, Callie stood her ground. "I'm not going, Dad."

To her relief, Rex stepped in front her. "Mr. Crowsen, I'm Rex Billings."

"I know who you are," Stuart growled. "Get out of my way." He came to a halt, however, in the middle of the road.

"My father is ill, sir. I have my hands full with the ranch. Until my sisters can get here, we need Callie's help."

"Get other help."

"I don't have time to find other help," Rex argued reasonably. "And Callie's agreed to work for us."

"She's my daughter, and she's coming home with me," Stuart insisted.

Rex widened his stance and folded his arms. It was the very pose that Bo had taken when he'd told Stuart that he and Callie were getting married. Callie had feared that the announcement would come to violence, but Bo had promised otherwise, and he had kept his word.

"You have no legal authority over Callie," Rex said.

"That's my granddaughter!" Stuart bawled, throwing out a finger.

"Do you have legal custody of her?" Rex asked.

"He doesn't," Callie answered quietly, her voice wavering.

Rex didn't so much as glance in her direction. He kept his focus on her father and his tone level. "You have no legal recourse here, Mr. Crowsen. I understand that you're upset, but Callie and Bodie are safe and comfortable. You have my word on it. Moreover, Callie is being handsomely paid."

That upset Stuart even more, though Rex wouldn't have understood that. "You stay out of this, Billings! Callie, you're coming home with me."

"No, Dad, I'm not," she said firmly, emboldened by Rex's support. "I've been telling you for a while now that Bodie and I need to make our own way."

Stuart thumped himself in the chest. He never wore anything but a white dress shirt with the sleeves rolled back and dark slacks.

"*I* provide for you," he declared. "You have no need to earn money."

"But I do," she told him softly. "I'm afraid the price for your provision is too high."

They both knew she was talking about Ben Dolent. Stuart heaved several deep breaths, considering his next move. She imagined that he was tallying up any loans that he held on the Billings' properties, any feed bills due, any equipment orders. The amount must have been negligible, for he shook his head and pointed a thick finger at her.

"I just want to take care of you, girl. Why won't you accept that I know what's best?"

"Why won't you accept that I'm a grown woman who can decide what's best for herself?"

Stuart shook his head. "I've worked my whole life to provide for you, Callie. You defied me once, and look what happened. I won't stand for this a second time!"

"I'm afraid you have no choice," Rex told him evenly. "My father is ill. I won't have him upset. Callie's already done him a world of good, and if she wants to stay, she's staying. I can make it official and get a protective order to keep you off the property, if you insist."

"You think a piece of paper will keep me away?" Stuart demanded.

Rex took a step forward, balling his hands into fists. "If it won't," he threatened, "I'm not above throwing you off the place myself. You think I can't, you come here raving like a madman again."

"I'm older than you by twenty years at least," Stuart pointed out, backing up a step.

"You are," Rex admitted, "but you look fit enough to me, and I'll make good on that threat if I have to."

Stuart glared, and snarled, "This isn't over," and stomped off to his big luxury car. He always drove the most expensive model of Cadillac.

Callie let out a silent breath of relief as he got inside, started the engine and drove away. Rex slid her a look from the corners of his eyes.

"Okay. Now I know why we won't be going back to his place for anything."

"He doesn't mean any harm," Callie said, tears filling her eyes, "and I don't want to hurt him. He just…" She didn't know how to explain her father's overbearing overprotectiveness. Shaking her head, she carried her daughter toward the ranch house.

Her heart still pounded, and she privately admitted she was thrilled at the way Rex had stood up to her father, but she couldn't help thinking that Bo would have handled it differently. Quiet, mild-mannered Bo had accomplished with sheer determination what Rex had done with threats and bravado. The thrill she'd felt when Rex had stepped between her and her father confused her. At least Rex hadn't told her to pack her things and leave with Stuart, though, and he'd made it plain that she was valued at Straight Arrow Ranch.

She wondered just how long Rex meant to

remain around War Bonnet. And that she even wondered worried her.

Stomping into the garage and throwing things calmed Rex somewhat, but he hated nothing more than a blustering bully. He'd had enough of that. When he'd walked away from his marriage and his job, he'd promised himself that he'd never put up with that kind of demanding, overbearing manipulation again.

Dennis Gladden had used his daughter as a bargaining chip. Rex had been foolish enough to believe that Amy loved him. He had married her in spite of who her father was, not because of it. Only later had he realized that Amy was meant to keep him in line, to bend him to her daddy's will. When Rex had refused to be molded into an obedient yes-man, Amy had transferred her affections to a more malleable candidate within the firm, with her father's approval. Rex still didn't know if his discovery of her infidelity had been conveniently orchestrated or if it had truly been an accident. Certainly Dennis had known that Amy was at his house on the river when he'd sent Rex there for a weekend of fishing to "consider the future." Whether Dennis had known that she was there with another man or not, Rex neither knew nor truly cared.

In a funny way, Amy and her bully of a father had made it possible for Rex to take care of his dad. He'd be hanged if another bully of a father would get in the way of that. He couldn't help wondering why Stuart Crowsen would be so adamant about his daughter not leaving his household, though. He could understand if he was so fond of her and little Bodie that he wanted them with him, but it wasn't as if they'd moved across the state. They hadn't gone half a dozen miles away. And it was only a temporary situation.

Rex knew he was going to have to find out what was behind all this, if only to keep it from impacting Wes, but he didn't feel sufficiently calm enough for that discussion until after he'd returned to the house, checked on his dad and cleaned up. By that time, Callie had supper on the table.

"Feels like Glory could come walking into the room any moment," Wes commented, leaning an elbow on the table beside his plate. "Thank you, Callie."

"My pleasure."

"But from now on, you sit yourself down at this table with us," Wes went on. "We take our meals together in this house."

Rex knew he should have thought of that, but she seemed to be constantly moving about the kitchen. The only time she'd paused had been when Wes had said the blessing over the meal. Callie cast a taut smile at Wes and nodded. A thin wail rose from the second floor of the house, and Callie immediately began to remove her apron. It had been one of his mom's favorites, sewn from remnants of her handmade clothing.

"That's another thing," Wes said to Rex, as she hurried toward the stairs. "There's an old high chair out in the storage room in the barn. Your mom was saving it for grandchildren, but seeing as none of you kids have been cooperative on that end, it'll do for Bodie. Probably needs some work."

"I'll see to it," Rex promised.

"You do that," Wes ordered. "Bringing those two here was a good thing, son."

"I hope so," Rex said. But he still had to ask Callie a question.

He got his chance a couple hours later. Wes was better, but he wasn't up to par. Rex had helped him sponge off, check the bandages on his incisions and dress for bed. Wes's willingness to let Rex help him was a testament to his exhaustion, which in turn showed that he still had a lot of recovery ahead of him.

Hearing Bodie babbling on the front porch, Rex walked out there to find Callie sitting in one of the chairs, holding Bodie's hands while the baby jogged up and down around her mom's knee, which sported a wide, wet spot where Bodie had drooled.

Bodie looked up at him, smiled and clearly said, "Hiii."

"Hi, cutie."

"She just started doing that," Callie informed him with a smile. "She won't say 'mama' yet, but she's suddenly saying, 'hi.' Of course, she has no idea what it means."

"Mmm," Bodie hummed against her mother's leg.

Rex walked around them both and sat down in the metal lawn chair next to Callie. It sagged and creaked ominously. He held his breath, but the chair seemed stable enough. With dusk settling around them, the stifling heat had begun to abate, but the only breeze stirring was that pulled in by the ceiling fan in the living room.

"I'll get someone out here to look at the AC unit tomorrow," he said. "According to Dad, it just needs coolant."

Callie nodded beside him and softly said, "Wes is going to need air-conditioning to get through his chemo. He doesn't think so, but I do. We're two hours farther south here than Tulsa. You know how brutal these summers can be. I hate to think of him being sick to his stomach in hundred-degree heat."

"I appreciate that," Rex said. "I should've taken care of it already."

"You've had other things on your mind."

"I have. There's something on my mind now."

"You want to know why my dad is so upset about me working for you."

"Yeah."

"Ben Dolent."

"Who?"

"Ben Dolent. He runs Dad's grain silo, and Dad has him picked out as his next son-in-law."

"I take it you're not in favor of the idea."

"No."

"What about your first husband? Did Stuart pick him, too?"

"Oh, no," Callie said, shaking her head and chuckling. "Bo was the exact opposite of the sort of man my dad wants me to marry."

"What sort of man would that be?" Rex asked.

"One he can control, I guess," Callie answered. "The kind who will do as he's told and be glad for it."

"And Bo wasn't that kind of man?"

"He wasn't." She curved her hand around Bodie's little head, smoothing the baby's pale hair. "Bo didn't care about money. He didn't care about status. All he cared about was me, us and serving God. He had a campground ministry over at Turner Falls. Didn't pay much. I had to work to make ends meet, but we had all we needed. For the little while we were together. We were only married a few months. He hadn't had time to put away anything for us."

"I'm sorry you lost him," Rex said.

She cleared her throat, her gaze on the baby. "I'm still trying to figure out what God's doing," she admitted softly, shaking her head. "I just don't understand yet. I worked and saved every penny right up until my labor started, but when Bodie was nine weeks old she got sick and couldn't go to day care, and that's all it took. We had to go back to my dad's. I know it was God's will. I just don't believe it's His will for me to marry Ben Dolent."

Rex didn't know what to say to that. His own marriage had imploded because his wife's father had wanted a son-in-law who would "do as he's told and be glad for it" and his wife had been only too happy to try to provide the same. When Rex had balked, the marriage had suffered. He'd sought refuge in work, thinking that if he could prove himself professionally then she would take pride in him. Instead, she'd gone to another man. He couldn't help thinking that they'd still be together if she'd had Callie's strength of character or if she'd loved him as much as Callie had apparently loved her husband.

He smiled at Bodie. "You named her after her father, didn't you?"

"Yes. Her father and my mother. Bodie Jane. It seemed appropriate. She'll never know her daddy, and I was only four when my mother died. I barely remember her."

"It's a good name," he said, getting to his feet, "and it's good that the two of you are here."

"I'm glad you think so, especially after the way my father acted today."

He did think so. A strong urge to put his hand on her shoulder seized him. He did it before he could stop the impulse, and the rightness of it shook him. Looking at his hand as it cupped her slender shoulder, he suddenly felt as if he hardly knew himself. The frayed cuff of his father's old work shirt and the sheer size of his hand against her smooth, firm, woman's frame rattled him. It was as if he'd never really seen his own hand before, never really touched a woman. He thought of Amy, and for a moment he wondered if she'd even been real. Shaking his head he took his hand away, thinking that he really needed to get some rest.

As for Callie Deviner, he was glad to have her help, but their arrangement was temporary, and even were it not, he had no intention of allowing history to repeat itself.

Pretty little Callie Deviner had the wrong sort of father.

Besides, once Wes was able to take over the reins of Straight Arrow Ranch again—or if it should be determined that Wes could never do so—Rex would be heading back to Tulsa. That's where his life and his career were based. For as long as Rex could remember, he'd dreamed of leaving War Bonnet and the Straight Arrow Ranch. He'd wanted no part of the backbreaking drudgery that was his father's life here, always at the mercy of the weather and whatever new disease befell the livestock or the crops.

No, this life, and any woman so obviously comfortable with this life, was not for him. That meant he would be wise to keep his distance from Callie.

"I'll say good-night," he told her.

"Good night."

"I'll, um, find that high chair in the morning."

"It's not important."

"I promised Dad."

"All right."

He reached down to smooth a hand over Bodie Jane's head. "Good night, precious."

"Hiii," she said.

Callie laughed and instructed her. "Bye-bye. Bye-bye."

"Buh-buh-buh-buh-buh."

Chuckling, Rex went into the house, said good-night to his father and climbed the stairs to read and wait for the dark that would bring him rest for another arduous day.

Chapter Four

The air conditioner repairman had to come all the way from Ardmore, so it would be late afternoon before he could reach them. Naturally, Friday turned up scorching hot before lunchtime. Wes fretted about the horses in the paddock beyond the stable barn.

"They need fresh bedding and the water troughs have to be cleaned, but I don't want to plague Rex with anything more just now," he told Callie when she brought him a tall glass of iced tea.

"Can't one of the ranch hands see to it?"

"There's only the three of them, and Rex has them working cattle today. Looks like a bumper crop of bull calves this year, and they've got to be castrated before the end of the month." He shot an embarrassed glance at Callie. "Sorry. That's blunt talk for a town girl."

Callie chuckled. "You forget that I grew up in the Feed and Grain. I've heard worse, believe me."

"All the same," he mumbled.

Callie puzzled on the situation for a moment, then asked, "Do you have a cell phone?"

The only landline in the house hung on the wall in the kitchen—and had a rotary dial. She wondered if the thing even worked. She'd seen Rex talking on his cell phone, so she knew they had coverage out here.

Frowning, Wes opened the drawer in his bedside table and began pawing through it. "Gotta be 'round here somewhere." Finally he came up with a flip phone that looked as if it had come right out of the package. "My girls call me every few days. Otherwise, I forget about the fool thing."

"May I?" Callie asked, holding out her hand. He dropped the small phone into it, and she quickly programmed in Bo's old number. They'd only had the one phone between them, and thankfully Bo hadn't been carrying it the day of the flash flood that had taken his life. She'd managed to maintain the line, though her father had wanted her to cancel it and replace it with a business phone. "Here's what we'll do," she said, handing back the phone. "I'll bring in that old playpen that Rex found in the storeroom this morning when he went looking for the high chair, and you can watch Bodie while I go out and take care of the horses."

"I can't let you do that," Wes protested, shifting on the bed.

"I've scrubbed out troughs before," she assured him, "and I'm sure I can manage to muck out a few stalls if you'll just explain how—"

"Although," he interrupted, his pale blue gaze taking on a thoughtful expression, "what you could do is just open the gates between the paddock and the corrals beside the big barn. It's shady over there, and if you turn the tap on and fill that trough next to the red barn, the horses will find their own way to it."

Callie smiled. "I can do that. You have to promise that you won't pick Bodie up while I'm gone, though. If she starts fussing, you just let her fuss. We can't risk you opening an incision. If you get worried about her, you can call me and I'll come right away. Agreed?"

He nodded and mused, "You know, when I built that paddock, there were three big trees in it, but the drought killed them, one by one, and I had to take them down. Now the horses have no shade out there, so they spend more time inside, which makes more work for us, but I can't let them suffer this heat without some sort of relief, especially my faithful Soldier. That old gentleman has carried me many a mile and bred up some fine animals. Not a better behaved stud in the state."

"I understand," Callie said. "Let me get things situated in here, and I'll open those gates."

"Thanks, Callie."

She made quick work of it, having already scrubbed every inch of the old wood playpen. The padding had long since disintegrated, so she folded a frayed, faded, quilted bedspread and put that in the bottom of the playpen, which she positioned next to Wes's bed, before hanging one of Bodie's favorite activity toys on the side rail and tossing in some stuffed animals. After feeding and changing Bodie, Callie retrieved the cell phone then plopped the baby down in the cushioned playpen and entertained her for several minutes with the activity center. While Bodie busily played with her toys, Callie slipped out to see to the horses.

She started by turning on the tap in the metal trough in the corral next to the big red barn, then wound her way through the maze of fences, opening the gates that led down to the horse paddock. Seeing only one animal in the pasture, it occurred to her that the others might be hiding from the heat in the horse barn, so she ventured in there.

The odors of horse, hay and manure enveloped her. As her eyes adjusted to the shadowed interior, she saw that all of the stall gates stood open so the horses could come and go as they pleased, but a glance at the nearest trough showed her why Wes was concerned. A green scum ringed the metal container.

Callie didn't know much about horses, but she knew better than to surprise them, so she started talking before she started walking. "Hey, now, fellas, it's cooler and cleaner up by the red barn, so why don't we take a walk?"

Just moving around with her arms held out seemed to be enough to get the first one headed toward the door. Another soon followed, and then a big, dark beauty lifted its head, blew through its nostrils and the remaining four horses went out the door in a rapid clip. Smiling, Callie went out a safe distance behind them. She had to climb over a couple fences to get near the water tap and turn it off without wading through horses. They obviously appreciated the fresh water and clean trough. She climbed over those same fences again to avoid skirting too close to swishing tails and rear hooves on her way back to the house, but as she hit the dirt next to the road, she found unwelcome help waiting.

Meaty hands reached out to steady her as

she landed after hopping backward from the top rail of the fence.

"Careful. Don't hurt yourself."

She'd know that oddly thin voice anywhere, and pulled away as politely as she could manage. "I'm fine."

"I thought you were keeping house and cooking for the Billingses," Ben Dolent said, squinting at her from above a stiff smile.

"That's right." She brushed her hands on the seat of her jeans and started for the house. "Need to get back and check on Wes and the baby."

"How is old Wes?" Ben asked, hurrying to keep up with her. He wasn't much taller than her, and his short legs meant that he had to take twice as many steps. She resisted the urge to lengthen her stride.

"Still weak but mending. He'll start chemo before long."

Ben clucked his tongue. He had a habit of doing that. "Terrible thing, cancer. I reckon Wes's daughters will want to nurse him through that."

"When they can," Callie said. "Right now, I'm it, though."

"You know you don't have to do this," Ben said, pumping his arms in an attempt to keep pace with her. "I'll gladly hire professional help for old Wes."

Callie felt her jaw drop. She came to a halt beneath the bur oak in the front yard and glared at him. "You'd cheat me out of my wages?"

Huffing for air, Ben threw up his hands, his round face registering shock and surprise. Obviously he hadn't considered all the ramifications when he'd agreed to this little ploy of Stuart's. "No! I—I just want to spare you the work."

"But I enjoy the work, Ben. And where would you find *professional* help around here?"

"There's an agency over in Lawton," he squawked as she turned and headed for the porch.

"That's over an hour away," she tossed over her shoulder.

"But they'll send help if it's live-in," he argued, following on her heels.

"To cook and clean *and* care for Wes?" she demanded, turning on him.

"Nursing care," he answered lamely, backing up a step.

"Wes doesn't need nursing right now as much as he needs good food, clean clothes and company," she declared. "Now, the Billings family have hired me, and I'm staying. That's all there is to it."

Ben lifted his chin, what there was of it. "Callie, listen to reason."

"You're not talking reason. You're saying what Stuart Crowsen has told you to say. Goodbye, Ben."

"I trust that's an end to it," she heard Rex say and turned to find him on the pathway behind them.

Ridiculously pleased, she stepped up onto the porch and went into the house without so much as a backward glance. She heard Ben and Rex speaking, but the conversation was short. She breathed a silent sigh of relief when she heard Ben's vehicle leave a few moments later.

Rex didn't mention the encounter, but after dinner she walked into the kitchen from Wes's room to find Rex waiting for her. He'd leaned a hip against the kitchen counter and waited with folded arms. When he saw her, he straightened and calmly announced, "You have company again."

Puzzled, she moved into the dining area, Rex following on her heels. When she saw Ben standing in the living room with a bouquet of flowers in one hand and his cowboy hat in the other, Callie didn't know who she most wanted to slap, Ben or Rex. Or her father.

Instead she kept her apron on, silently prayed

for patience, smiled and said, "Why, Ben. How nice. These must be for the patient."

Ben looked blindsided as she took the flowers from his hand. "Uh…"

"I'll put these in water and see if Wes is up to visitors."

She left him standing in the living room with Rex, who seemed to be trying not to laugh as he rocked back on his heels.

As she took down a large jar and arranged the flowers in it—they were the same ones she'd seen in the grocery a couple days earlier—silence stretched thin in the other room. Finally, Rex spoke.

"Dad's usually pretty tired after he's eaten. Just coming to the table takes a lot out of him, but at least he's doing that now, and I'm sure he'd want to thank you personally for the flowers."

"Oh. Uh. I don't want to bother him," Ben muttered. "Just…wanted him to know I'm thinking of him."

"That's very good of you," Rex said carefully.

Callie bit her lip and stayed right where she was. After a moment fraught with uncertainty, Ben mumbled about calling again sometime and left. Callie didn't move a muscle until she heard the screen door slam behind him. Only then did she creep to the doorway between the kitchen and dining area to peek out. Rex stood just on the other side, his arms folded.

"So that's your boyfriend, huh?" Rex teased.

She glared at him. "Do not call him that, even as a joke."

Rex grinned, splitting the beard-shadowed lower half of his face with the blindingly white crescent of his smile. "Poor guy's fighting way out of his class."

The compliment pleased her, which was exactly why she didn't even acknowledge it.

"Why did you let him in?"

"What did you expect me to do? When he asked me this afternoon if you and I are 'getting together,' I told him no. I didn't imagine he'd take that as permission to come courting."

She sighed, her face flaming. "I'm sorry. He had no right to ask you that."

"Seems a reasonable question," Rex said in a low voice. "I'd want to know if I was him."

She shook her head. "I've told him over and over again that I'm not interested in him, but my father just keeps sending him after me."

"Obviously your father is the one you have to convince."

"Don't you think I've tried?" she demanded. "He just insists that Ben will take care of me and Bodie if something happens to him, as if I can't be trusted to take care of the two of us." Wincing, she admitted, "I guess my record isn't too good, but it's still infuriating and appalling. I have to prove to my father that I can provide for me and my daughter."

"Okay," Rex said, turning back toward the living room. "I get it. Your wildly overprotective father wants you settled with a man he knows will provide for you the way he wants you provided for. You don't want the man he's chosen and are intent on proving that you can provide for your daughter on your own."

"That about sums it up." Except for the part where her dad would go to extremes to get his way. She just hoped, prayed, that Wes Billings had been smart enough to stay out of Stuart Crowsen's grasp.

The repaired baler lasted all of one day in the field then broke a drive chain. Rex called in to town to see if Crowsen had a replacement. To his surprise, not only did the Feed and Grain have the part, Crowsen offered to have it delivered at once. Rex agreed to receive the delivery at the house and should not have been surprised when Dolent arrived with the drive chain, though why the manager of the grain silo would be delivering equipment parts could not have been more evident, especially when he asked to go into the house for a drink of water. Rex offered him iced tea from the thermos that Callie had filled for him that morning, but Dolent apparently *craved* water.

Dolent did not discourage easily; Rex would give him that. Unfortunately, the man didn't appear bright enough to realize that he had zero chance with a woman like Callie.

Even though time was of the essence, Rex walked Dolent inside, insisted he take a moment to say hello to Wes and walked Dolent out again, with nothing more than a cool drink and a glimpse of Callie, who was busy preparing lunch. He made sure Ben saw the flowers in the jar on the dresser in Wes's room. Then he gave Ben a hearty handshake and his sincere thanks before all but physically tossing the dullard into the Crowsen Feed and Grain pickup truck.

Obviously frustrated, Dolent started up the engine, backed the truck up and drove away, but Rex stood where he was until the pickup disappeared from view. Callie had sent him a look of thanks when he'd steered Ben out of the kitchen, and Rex privately admitted to some personal irritation mixed with his amusement over the man's dogged persistence. Surely even Ben would soon get the message: Callie was not for him.

The fact that she was not for Rex, either, was beside the point.

That didn't keep Rex from worrying that Dolent might be at the house making a nuisance of himself while he was out in the field trying to replace the drive chain on the baler. He finally decided that he didn't have the proper tools to repair the baler in the field. Hot, tired, disgusted and frustrated, Rex hitched the thing to the ranch truck and hauled it back to the barn.

He thought Callie might come out to see what was up, but she seemed as determined to keep her distance from him as he ought to keep his distance from her. At least Dolent wasn't within sight.

Rex left the baler in the barn and called an early end to the workday. It was Saturday, after all. Not that work on the ranch ever let up.

He walked into the house to find two things that shocked him: it was cool, and Callie had just pushed Wes into the living room in the hated wheelchair that he'd vowed never to use.

"Pick your jaw up off the floor," Wes grumbled. "I got sick of that bed, but the living room is a long way from my bedroom. Besides, Callie pointed out that I could get to church tomorrow if I was willing to give this chair a go."

Rex had not intended to take his father to

church this Sunday, but if doing so was the cost of getting him out of that bed more often and into this chair, so be it. Telegraphing his thanks to Callie with a smile, Rex nodded. Bodie let out a squeal from the other room, and Wes chuckled as Callie hurried to tend to her.

"That girl never stops hopping. Reminds me of when you kids were small." He looked up at Rex and asked, "Got time for a game of chess before dinner?"

"Just let me clean up first," Rex answered.

"Sure." Wes picked up the TV remote from the coffee table at his knee and aimed it at the big flat-screen that Rex and his sisters had bought him for Christmas last year.

Rex hurried to the stairs, but a few steps up he paused to look down on the familiar scene below. Cowhide rugs covered plank flooring. The oak occasional tables, at least fifty years old, stood as solid and strong as ever. The leather on the old couch had started to crack in places, and his father's recliner, easily the newest piece in the room, sagged and dipped. The shades on the glass and wrought-iron lamps had yellowed horribly, as had the blinds on the windows. Yet, the room exuded comfort and stability.

Home, he thought, stunned by the realization. Even after all these years, this was still home in a way that the luxury condo he owned in Tulsa never could be. Everything here said *home* to him, from the rugged cross hanging over the fireplace to the schoolhouse clock and candelabra on the mantel. Funny, it hadn't felt that way before Callie had come.

Shaking his head, he climbed the stairs. For the first time, he faced the possibility of what might happen to the place if Wes could never resume control of the day-to-day operations. The Straight Arrow would essentially cease to exist. They'd have to sell off the acreage in order to pay the taxes on the home place, the house and the few acres surrounding it. But for whom? After Wes, who would live here?

Rex hoped to have children of his own someday, but he wasn't getting any younger. Thirty-seven wasn't too old to start a family, of course, and when he did finally have his own children they surely might have some interest in this place. That they might not seemed... unthinkable suddenly. Unbearable.

He wondered why he hadn't realized it before now.

Later he played chess with his dad while Callie puttered around the kitchen and moved in and out of the living room, carrying Bodie. They enjoyed another fine meal together, and afterward Callie played quietly with Bodie on the floor while he and Wes watched television. Then she put the baby to sleep, and he listened to her moving about the house until she, too, turned in for the night. Wes went to bed as soon as his program ended. Rex sat up alone, listening to the TV and worrying about his father, only to dream of Callie when he finally did sleep and woke the next morning thinking of his mother and church.

It had been some time since Rex had attended church with any regularity, but Countryside had been good to his parents, and he'd happily fellowship there. He put on a suit and tie even before he headed downstairs for breakfast. Adjusting the knot in his tie, Rex looked at his image in the spotty mirror over the dresser in his bedroom.

His mom had finally removed the school logos and sports posters from the walls, but the rodeo-themed curtains and bedcovers remained. Once upon a time, his chief ambition in life had been to make a name for himself in rodeo. His father had wisely insisted that he do so *after* college. The urge hadn't survived his first semester at Oklahoma University. Eventually he'd given up his jeans for a suit, but the boots…well, those had just gotten more expensive. He wouldn't know how to walk in shoes. He did know how to turn down the collar on a shirt made especially for him and shrug into a jacket tailored to his exact measurements.

The suit jacket hung a little loose around his middle now. No surprise there. He'd had to take up his belt a notch when he'd pulled on his pants this morning.

He picked up a brush and swept back his thick brown hair. It wasn't as dark as it had been even a week ago. He needed to remember to wear a hat. He still had a pair of them in the closet.

Strapping on his wristwatch, he checked the time. Better get a move on. Wes would need help dressing, and loading Wes and his wheelchair into the truck would take a few extra minutes. He went out along the hallway to the stairs. Before his foot took the first step down, Callie came out of her room with Bodie in her arms.

He could do nothing but stare at the wholesome beauty of her. She wore a spring-green dress, simple and sleeveless with a gently flared skirt and modestly scooped neckline. Bodie wore the same white sandals as her mom and a delicate pink-and-white striped dress over ruffled bloomers.

"I don't know which one of you looks more adorable," he said. Callie dropped her gaze, a delicate blush coloring her cheeks.

"That would be Bodie," she said in a playful voice, jostling her daughter. "Thank you."

He stepped back, waving a hand for her and the baby to go first. "You're welcome."

She reached inside her room and snagged a large handbag before hurrying onto the stairs. "You, um, clean up well."

Surprised—and ridiculously pleased—he slid a hand over his diminished middle, confiding, "Lost a little weight."

"Working in the heat will do that."

"No kidding. It will also fry your brain."

She laughed, but whatever she might have said got lost in the sound of knocking at the front door. Tossing a glance over her shoulder at Rex, Callie hurried downstairs. He joined her in the entryway, just as she pulled open the carved oak door.

"Dolent," Rex said, hoping he didn't sound as disgusted as he felt.

At the same time she exclaimed, "Ben!"

The squat silo manager stood there in a too-large, too-pale Western suit and a tan beaver cowboy hat. What looked like a brand-new Bible was folded against his chest in one chubby fist.

"I come to take you to church," he announced happily. "I know you'll want to go to your own church in town."

"No," Callie said flatly, her hand still on the door.

Dolent's smile faltered. "But you don't ever miss church. Your husband was a minister, wasn't he?"

"He was," Callie said. Surprised, Rex glanced at her and back at Dolent. "That's not the point."

"I don't understand," Dolent whined.

"I'll be attending with the Billings family from now on," Callie explained.

"But—"

"Wes might need me," she said, starting to close the door, "but thanks, anyway."

"Wait!" Dolent insisted. "What if he's too sick to go to church?"

"I'll make sure she gets there," Rex heard himself say. Callie's shoulders lowered, as if she relaxed, and he stepped closer, grasping the edge of the door above her hand. Bodie reached for it, too, but her arm was much too short, so she touched Rex's arm instead. Somehow reassured by that tiny hand damp with drool, he promised, "Even if Wes is too ill to attend church, I'll see to it that Callie and Bodie get there."

Callie shifted, bringing her back into the lightest contact possible with his upraised arm. Rex felt that contact all the way into his chest.

"You shouldn't have come, Ben," Callie said

gently but firmly, "not without calling first. I could've saved you the trip if you'd just called."

Ben Dolent looked as if he might explode. Or cry.

Suddenly, without another word, he spun on his heels and hurried across the porch.

"Bye-bye," Bodie said, waving the damp hand with which she'd touched Rex.

Rex pushed the door closed, just in case Callie might be thinking better of it. She bowed her head then slowly turned and looked up at him.

"I feel like I just kicked a puppy."

"A puppy that needs some training."

Callie smiled. "True. By the way, thank you."

"For?"

"Promising to take us to church regularly."

"Ah. No problem."

She nodded, giving him one of those small, close-lipped smiles of hers. The problem with that particular smile was that it increasingly made him want to kiss her, and *that* was not part of the plan.

Unfortunately, for a moment, he couldn't remember just what the plan was supposed to be.

Oh, yeah. He was heading back to Tulsa as soon as his dad could take over the ranch again.

Well, in the meantime it wouldn't kill him to attend church regularly while he was here. He could think of worse things, much worse things, especially with Callie smiling beside him.

Chapter Five

"Sleep, baby girl."

Callie tucked the featherweight blanket lightly around Bodie's relaxed form, knowing that the child would likely kick it off within the next ten minutes but unable to resist the instinct to cover her. Fed, dry and exhausted from a morning of new faces and experiences at Countryside Church, Bodie slept deeply. Wes, too, slumbered after the midday meal. Callie would gladly have joined them, but Rex had gone out to the barn to tackle the baler again, saying that he dared not lose another day before getting it back into the field.

Stuart was religious about keeping the Sabbath, but Bo, being in ministry, had found it necessary to work on Sundays, and Callie had noticed that her father never seemed to mind that *she* labored on Sundays to provide his meals and make him comfortable. As Bo had said, *One person's labor may honor another's Sabbath, while holiness comes from the heart.*

She went downstairs, dropped several mint leaves into a quart jar, added ice cubes and a cup of apple juice, then filled it the rest of the way with unsweetened tea. Taking a pair of apples with her, she walked out to the barn.

Rex had the baler jacked up so high that it practically lay on its side. His shirt off, he was using a come-along, or wire stretcher, to slip the drive chain onto the baler. Those shoulders were even broader than she'd realized. Flustered, she placed the apples on the workbench and cleared her throat, but Rex was too busy to notice.

"Brought you something cold."

Rex spun around. She dropped her gaze, but not before she glimpsed smooth muscle. From the corner of her eye, she saw Rex reach for the chambray shirt he'd draped over the fender of the baler. Hearing snaps closing and steps scuffing, she held out the jar. Only after he took it from her hand did she lift her gaze. He brought the jar to his lips and drank deeply, tilting back his head.

"Oh, man, that's good," he said, holding the jar to his forehead.

"Need some help?"

He looked at her blue T-shirt, jeans and canvas shoes, then down at his greasy hands. "You sure?"

She nodded. "I can get all the way under there. You can't. Smart idea, by the way, using the come-along. There's a special tool for that, though."

"Well, if we've got one, I couldn't find it," he said before taking another long drink.

"This'll work. Just don't let that thing slip and hit me."

He grinned. "Don't worry. I'm not about to risk my best employee."

Chuckling, she held out her hand. "Got the pulley pin?"

He fished it out of his pocket and handed it to her, saying, "You've done this before."

"I have." Crouching, she crawled under the baler. It was dark, dirty and smelled of oil, gasoline and alfalfa. "Hay smells green."

"Yeah. Means we've still got a couple weeks to get it in. We're going to need it."

"Got a flashlight? I'm blocking what light there is under here."

"Hold on."

She heard him rummaging around. After a minute or two, he passed her a heavy-duty flashlight.

She went to her knees, eased her upper body into the workings of the machine and shone a light on the chain, following it.

"I don't know how you did," she told him, "but it looks great. You've got a couple loose bolts here, though, and they need tightening before we lock this chain. Pass me an adjustable wrench."

"Yes, ma'am."

Before they got all the adjustments made, he had to go to his back on the ground while she held the light with one hand and guided him with the other to get the wrench properly placed and the necessary bolt effectively tightened. Finally, Callie was ready to put the pin in place.

After working several minutes, she finally had to admit that, while she could get the pin in the hole, she couldn't push it flat. "I'm just not strong enough."

Rex tried to reach the small metal peg but his big hand wouldn't fit into the space available. "If I just had a pair of pliers with really long handles," he mused. Suddenly he started scrambling out from under the baler, saying, "I have an idea."

Callie heard him rummaging around in the toolbox and muttering to himself. He returned a minute or so later, pulling on his work gloves.

He'd fixed a pair of vise grips to each handle of a pair of locking pliers, effectively extending the pliers by several inches. Realizing what he meant to do, Callie put her head next to his and shone the light on the exact spot where the pliers needed to grip. He closed the pliers and squeezed the vise grips with big, strong hands, straining the muscles in his arms, shoulders and neck.

"Aaahhhh!" He fell back, letting his arms drop. "That's all I can do." He loosened the pliers and removed then. "Was it enough?"

She shone the light on the pin and studied. "Perfect. I can't even see the pin."

Sighing, Rex patted her hand with his gloved one. "Let's get out from under here." He tossed away the pliers before rolling out from under the baler and into a sitting position. Callie crawled out on her elbows and knees.

"What would I do without you?" Rex asked, folding his legs and balancing his forearms on his thighs.

Thrilled more than was wise, Callie got up and went to the workbench, retrieving the pliers on the way. She traded the pliers, vise grips and the flashlight for the apples, which she carried back to Rex. When she offered an apple to him, he took it with a chuckle, tossing it lightly before biting into it. Callie went down on her knees again then sank into a sitting position, her legs curled to one side.

"I could say the same about you," she told him. "This job gives me a way out of my situation, and your promise to take me to church closes one more avenue for Ben to plague me."

He shook his head and asked, "What is the deal with Dolent?"

She sighed. "He believes whatever my father tells him."

"So no matter how many times you tell him no, as long as Stuart keeps encouraging him, he'll keep showing up."

"I'm afraid so."

"I don't get it," Rex said. "Why would Stuart want you with a clod like that?"

Callie turned her apple over in her hands. "I defied Dad once and married against his wishes, and Dad seems to believe that Bo's death is a direct result of that defiance. All I can figure is that he's determined to keep me from making what he sees as another mistake by insisting that I marry someone he can control."

"How did your husband die?" Rex asked gently, looking at her from beneath the crag of his brow.

"He drowned," Callie said softly. "We operated a Christian youth encampment at Turner Falls. There was a flash flood, the first in decades."

His brow furrowed, Rex said, "I heard about that. I thought nearly everyone got out safe. I read that some fellow got a family out of a car and was washed away…trying to save a child." Callie bowed her head, smiling even as tears filled her eyes. "They hailed him as a hero," Rex finished slowly.

"That was my Bo," she whispered. "They found him holding that baby. She was three. They're buried side by side."

"Callie, I'm so sorry."

She nodded, but then she smiled and said. "I'm not. He was a good man, and he did the right thing. He made me happy and proud. Now I have to do the right thing by his daughter, even if my dad doesn't understand."

"I don't understand why Stuart is so against you working."

"He isn't against me working. I work all the time in his businesses. He's against me earning my own money. Because he knows that Bodie and I will move away from War Bonnet when I have the means to do so."

"You said Bo didn't leave you anything."

"Not even the money to bury him with,"

she confided. "There wasn't time. We weren't married even six months."

"That's tough."

"God provided. People were very good. A local funeral home donated their services. The family who lost their little girl paid for the plot. Area churches chipped in to buy a headstone. People all over the state sent money to help repair the campgrounds. My ob-gyn even donated his services when he learned what happened, but full-time day care is so expensive, and the couple weeks I had to take off when she was born put me behind. Then she got sick, and I had to take off work again. My only option seemed to be to move back to my father's house. I knew getting out again would be difficult. I just didn't figure on Ben Dolent."

"So you want to leave town," Rex said, shifting closer.

"Not really." She shook her head. "War Bonnet's my home. But I have no choice. No one will give me steady, paying work here. They're too afraid of my dad. So I've got to go somewhere else."

"I see."

"We won't go far," she told him. "Ringling, maybe, or Comanche, someplace where Stuart Crowsen doesn't have his finger in every pie."

"Those are still small towns," Rex pointed

out, "not much bigger than War Bonnet, probably less than two thousand people."

"Small-town life is what I want for my girl," Callie said. "It's what her daddy wanted for her. I'll try Duncan or Ardmore, if I can't find work in a smaller town."

"Neither is exactly a metropolis," Rex noted. "What are their populations? Twenty-five thousand, tops? There are more students at the University of Oklahoma."

"That seems pretty big to me," Callie admitted. "Just think of it. You could live there your whole life and not know a tenth of the people."

"Never thought of it that way," Rex admitted, frowning.

She changed the subject, polishing her apple on her thigh. "What did you think of the church service this morning?" Taking a big bite, she waited for him to do the same.

"It was different."

"How so?"

"First time I've ever seen the pastor play guitar in the praise band."

She laughed. "He's pretty good."

"He is, on the guitar and in the pulpit."

Callie nodded. "Folks aren't so concerned about appearances at Countryside. They enjoy worship. I'm all for reverence, but I think God has a sense of fun, too."

"He must. There was lots of laughter out there this morning, and I got the feeling that's the norm."

"I hope so," Callie said, getting to her feet. "Better go check on my sleepers now."

"I'll be in shortly," Rex said, following suit. "Thanks again, Callie."

She nodded and started to walk away, but then she stopped and turned back. "Just so you know, this job, you, you're an answered prayer for me."

Rex opened his mouth, and for a moment she thought he might speak, but then he bowed his head, and she went on, strangely pleased and, for the moment at least, at peace.

Answered prayer. When on God's green earth had he ever been such a thing for anyone else? The idea shamed Rex. Callie Deviner shamed Rex. She worked daylight to dark without ever uttering a word of complaint. Just the opposite, in fact. She worked hard *and* was downright pleasant about it. Wes loved her. She'd made a huge difference around here and earned every cent of her pay.

Moreover, Rex was man enough to admit that the heartbreak she'd endured would have destroyed him. He could barely imagine how alone and helpless she must have felt when her husband had died. In his own case, anger and hurt pride had overshadowed any pain or sense of loss that he'd felt at Amy's betrayal, and that told him an uncomfortable truth about his past marriage.

He spent a long night in contemplation, coming to the conclusion that he and Amy simply had not loved each other the way Callie and her husband had. Maybe that would have changed over time, but somehow Rex doubted it. He sensed something clean and honest about the way Callie and Bo had loved, something he'd never felt with Amy.

He'd always known that kind of love had thrived between his parents, but somehow he'd thought it was a thing of the past, something that no longer existed in this modern world. Callie made him feel ten times the fool and out of sync with this place and time. Worse, she made him feel…*lonely.* For something he hadn't even known he was missing. That left him unsettled and agitated.

A part of him longed for what his father and Callie seemed to have—a simpler, truer way of life, an easier way of seeing the world. Another part of Rex couldn't wait to get out of War Bonnet, leave Straight Arrow Ranch behind and return to the city and the practice of law with one of the more prestigious firms in Tulsa. This time, his goals would be different, however. This time he'd be less concerned with climbing the corporate ladder and leaving his personal mark and more concentrated on finding the right woman and building the right kind of life.

The right woman had to be out there. Callie proved it. She'd already stood up to her father in more ways that his ex ever would. She had put her man first and even now she honored him. Plus, she was a great mom, a wonderful homemaker and partner—for someone who meant to hang around War Bonnet, which he did not. Didn't he?

Somehow, he wasn't sure anymore. Just thinking of that old baler, he felt a surge of frustration—and an odd satisfaction that he studiously refused to examine. Instead, he got up and trudged through another busy day.

One thing about ranch life was that it never lacked for work to be done, even on a holiday. It also had more than its fair share of irritants: heat, dust, insects, cockleburs, cattle that showed up where they weren't supposed to be, hired hands who thought it was funny to hide bloody calf testicles in his cap when he wasn't looking so that he went in to lunch with smelly hair and had to dunk his head in the water trough before he could even sit down to eat. He had to throw the cap away and get out his old straw cowboy hat. It fit more comfortably than he'd imagined it would.

Callie showed him absolutely no compassion. "Finally blooded you, did they?"

"Aw, they're just excited about getting the afternoon off. I should've known something was up when they showed up on Memorial Day. Not like it's even the first time they've got me."

"It's been a while," Wes pointed out. "You were twelve the last time, if I recall."

Remembering, Rex grinned. "Woody dropped a fresh pair in my shirt pocket. I kept them and later hid them in his truck, where they went undiscovered for the whole weekend."

Callie winced, and Wes laughed. "As I recall, you wound up cleaning that truck cab with a toothbrush."

"More than once," Rex confirmed, grinning. "It still stunk."

A knock at the front door curbed their laughter. Callie touched Rex's shoulder, saying, "I'll go. Eat your lunch."

Assuming it was one of the men, he set about building himself a sandwich. When Callie returned, it was with Ben Dolent, her hands clasped together at her waist. Dolent carried a pale blue envelope and a vacuous smile. Doffing his hat, he spoke to Wes.

"Mr. Billings, it good to see you up and about."

"Thanks." He nodded at the blue envelope, asking, "What's this about, Ben?"

"Oh, it's purely a courtesy call," he said. "Mr. Crowsen understands how things can slip your mind in the midst of a health crisis, so he had me hand deliver this reminder to you." Beaming, he passed the envelope to Wes.

Splitting a loaded glance between Callie and Rex, Wes opened the envelope and removed a single slip of paper. After briefly reading, he tossed the paper and envelope onto the table.

"This note isn't due for sixty days, and you had to come out on Memorial Day to deliver it?"

Dolent shifted his feet. "Mr. Crowsen just wants you to know he's thinking about you."

Wes linked his fingers over his belt and hung an elbow on the edge of the table. "Well, you tell Stu Crowsen not to worry about his little note. It'll be paid in full and on time." He speared Dolent with a pointed glare then, adding, "But not one day before it's due. You tell him that."

Dolent's smile faded, replaced by uncertainty. "Um. Okay."

Rex picked up the slip and looked at it. Two thousand dollars. Crowsen was hounding them over two thousand dollars, sixty days before it was due? He looked at Callie, who had closed her eyes and bowed her head. Not hardly. Tossing the paper onto the table, Rex pushed up to his full height and seized Dolent by the arm.

"I think you're done here."

"What?" Dolent shot a glance at Callie. "I was hoping—"

"Nope," Rex interrupted, propelling the other man back the way he'd come. "You've done what you were sent to do."

"Listen," Dolent hissed, letting himself be escorted through the dining room and into the living area. "Wasn't my idea to come here like this."

"No, but you came," Rex growled.

"Because I wanted to see Callie."

"She doesn't want to see you."

"I'm trying to tell you that the boss can make life uncomfortable for you if he's of a mind to."

"Now, you listen to me," Rex muttered, holding on to his temper by a hair as he steered Dolent into the foyer. "I hate bullies." He turned Dolent to face him, stating flatly, "If Crowsen comes after my father or his daughter, I will use every weapon at my disposal to stop him."

He poked Dolent in the chest with the tip of his forefinger. "You got that?"

Dolent frowned and nodded. "I'm just trying to help."

"If you want to help," Rex said, "leave Callie alone and convince Stuart to do the same."

"She's his daughter," Dolent said, setting his mouth in a firm line. "He's got a right to try to take care of her."

"She's a grown woman," Rex said. "Crowsen has no legal rights where she is concerned. You tell him that."

Frowning, Dolent tapped the crown of his hat with a plump hand and pulled open the front door. Rex shut it behind him, sucked in a deep breath and tamped down his fury before returning to the kitchen.

"I'm so sorry," Callie said as he dropped down onto his chair again.

"Not your fault."

Wes waved a hand over his sandwich. "Stuart's just making noise. He can't hurt us. We don't need the Crowsen silos because we don't grow cash crops. We don't truly need the Feed and Grain because we raise most of our own fodder. The only loans he carries for us are small, good-neighbor loans that we can easily pay off. I just took them out because it's good business to support my local bank. Don't you worry, Callie, honey."

"I just don't want to cause trouble for you," Callie said miserably.

"We can protect our own," Rex told her, smearing mustard on a slice of bread. As far as he was concerned, that included her now.

He glanced up in time to see the worried tears in her eyes before she turned away and went back to work. Like her, he sensed that Stuart wasn't done, but he knew that Crowsen could do little where Straight Arrow Ranch and the Billings family were concerned.

Rex also knew that he would fight with everything in him to keep her here. Where she belonged.

Chapter Six

Rex spent the afternoon weeding his mother's flowerbed. It seemed an appropriate activity for Memorial Day. Callie came out to help him while Wes watched from his bedroom, Bodie playing in her playpen at the foot of his bed.

"I've been meaning to do this for a while," Rex said to Callie, pulling grass from among the peonies. Why was it the grass wouldn't grow elsewhere beneath the trees? "Just haven't taken the time."

On her knees a little distance away, Callie shook back her bangs. "You've been busy."

"Yep. That and…" He didn't know why he felt compelled to confess these things to her, but he did. "I used to help my mom do this. Makes me miss her."

"I understand that."

"I know you do."

They shared a wan smile and got back to cleaning out the bed. Afterward, they spread fresh straw over the bed to keep the weeds at bay. Then Wes asked to drive out to the cemetery to visit Gloria's grave. The old cemetery sat over five miles to the east and south of town, while the Straight Arrow lay more than a mile farther to the north and east. Wes asked Callie to come along, so she and the baby rode in the backseat of the truck while Rex drove and Wes hung his elbow out the open passenger window, basking in the heated air that rushed through the vehicle. Bodie seemed to enjoy the wind. Callie repeatedly combed her bangs with her fingers, smiled in that quiet, indulgent way of hers and occasionally met Rex's gaze in the rearview mirror.

He wondered if she felt the same electric jolt he felt when their gazes met. They certainly seemed to be developing a silent method of communication. He had merely glanced at the irises blanketing the foundation of the house, and Callie had gone to cut and tie them into bundles with white ribbons while Rex had placed Wes's wheelchair into the bed of the truck. It turned out that they didn't need the chair. Despite finding half a dozen other vehicles in the small, overgrown cemetery, Rex was able to pull the truck to a spot within a few yards of his mom's grave.

Wes had installed a granite bench there next to a lilac bush, which had grown large enough to provide shade. The bush hung heavy with blossoms browning in the heat, their fragrance filling the now-still air. Rex walked Wes to the bench and laid one of the iris bundles at the base of his mom's headstone while Callie carried Bodie and the second bundle to her mom's grave.

Stuart had placed a life-size statue of a woman with long hair seeming to launch herself heavenward from a recumbent position on a carved pedestal atop Mrs. Crowsen's grave. It looked pretentious and out of place in the humble little cemetery. Callie laid the bundle of irises on the platform, traced the lettering there with her fingertip, spoke quietly to her daughter and then began to stroll beneath the shade trees, Bodie in her arms as usual. Rex forced his gaze away from her in order to groom his mother's grave.

No wonder Ben Dolent was so taken with her. But what made him or Stuart think that she would have any interest in a mindless puppet like Ben? She'd married a bona fide hero the first time around, a real man's man apparently and a minister, no less. Why would she then settle for an older, unattractive dolt ready to do her overbearing father's every bidding? It would take a special man to replace Bo Deviner. That thought alone should have cowed Dolent. It somehow depressed Rex, not that he had any intention of going after the pretty widow himself.

Wes seemed wiped out by the short trip to the cemetery, but to Rex's relief, he rallied quickly. After a nap, he walked to the dinner table with more vigor than Rex had seen for some time, then ate a very hearty meal.

"The last of the stitches come out tomorrow," Rex reminded him.

"Callie can take me," Wes suggested.

Rex looked to Callie, who shrugged and nodded.

"Okay. Gives me a full day in the field. I hope."

"Provided the baler doesn't break down again, you mean," Wes said dryly.

"It won't," Callie said, scrubbing the tabletop with a soapy sponge. "And if it does, we'll fix it." They hadn't even left the table yet and the kitchen was already spotless.

Why did so many people find housework demeaning or unsatisfying when it was so essential to the comfort and well-being of a family? He and Amy had paid for domestic help, though Amy had not worked outside the home, despite having a degree in business management. She had complained about being bored and how the housekeeper did everything. Rex couldn't imagine Callie being bored. She was the most active, engaged woman he had ever known, except perhaps for his mom.

Amy had always quietly disdained the homemade goodies and gifts that his mother had sent their way. Rex had tried not to take offense, given Amy's background. Now he was ashamed that he hadn't taken *more* offense.

He almost pitied Amy. Her father had divorced her mother, married a younger woman and laughingly called it "trading up." A gifted attorney in her own right, Amy's mother, Chloe, had preached that every woman should be able to make her own way in the world, but in some ways Callie seemed better prepared to do that than either Amy or Chloe. Callie, after all, was the one standing up to her overbearing father and making an independent move, while Chloe's law practice depended on Amy's father even now and Amy seemed interested only in marrying to further his control of the firm.

Bodie, who was more fussy than usual, shoved her toy off the tray of the high chair and reached for her mother, complaining loudly.

"Muhmuhmuhmuhmuh."

Callie rinsed her hands, pulled a small tube from her hip pocket, squeezed a clear gel onto her fingertip and began to rub it onto Bodie's gums. "Those teeth are being stubborn, aren't they?"

She swung Bodie up out of the high chair and started for the stairs. The urge to follow hit Rex with stunning force. It took the breath right out of his body. What that was about, he couldn't even begin to guess.

Wes smiled and softly said, "You were a terror with those first teeth. Screamed like a banshee day and night. And your ma wasn't nearly that calm, you being her first. She was better with the girls. With you, she had her mother over here constantly, and my own mother lived here in the house with us." He chuckled. "Those were some tense days."

"I don't know where Callie gets her expertise and confidence," Rex said. "She didn't have a mother to guide her."

"All I know is," Wes told him, "that girl is a blessing."

A blessing, indeed. A blessing that was quickly becoming a personal problem for Rex.

Callie drove Wes into town on Tuesday to see the general practitioner. Dr. Alice Shorter divided her practice between several small towns in the area, so she kept office hours in War Bonnet only two days a week. Fifty-ish and no-nonsense, she wore rimless glasses over her dark brown eyes and kept her blond-streaked, light brown hair in a neat chignon. Callie had found her competent and friendly.

Wes seemed downright eager to see the doctor and get the last of his stitches removed. They arrived early, having the first appointment of the morning, and he walked into the clinic on his own, straight and tall. Dr. Shorter seemed as keen to see Wes as he was to see her. She stood at the reception desk, arms folded, waiting for him, and greeted him the moment he came through the door.

"Still breathing then, are you, Billings?"

"Still breathing, Shorter."

"So has that God of yours healed you yet?"

"That's what He's got you for."

Rolling her eyes, the doctor waved him past the desk and into an examination room. As she settled down with Bodie in the waiting area, Callie traded bemused looks with the young female receptionist. Someone else walked through the door just then, and that started a steady stream of patients. Wes returned, moving gingerly, about forty minutes after they'd arrived. Bodie was on the verge of a meltdown, fussing and bowing her back. Callie had risen to walk the floor with her and was about to take her outside when Wes appeared.

"Sorry for the delay," he said sheepishly, pushing the door open for her with one hand. In the other he carried a bag of what appeared to be samples from the doctor's stores.

"It really wasn't that long. Bodie's just in a foul mood. I'll give her a cold teething ring when we get home."

"Poor baby. Those teeth are really hurting her."

Callie belted the baby into her car seat while he eased along the sidewalk and into the passenger seat of the truck. When Callie climbed into the driver's seat next to him, he offered another apology.

"I should've gotten us out of there quicker. The doc and I have this running battle going, see, and I just can't resist debating with her," Wes explained. "She's mad at God because her husband died and all her training couldn't stop it. I keep asking her how she can be so mad at someone she claims not to believe in."

"Ah. Now I know how to pray about this."

Wes smiled. "That's the ticket. You and me, we're gonna pray her right into the Kingdom."

Callie nodded as she started up the truck. "And it starts with getting you well."

"I'll go for that," Wes said, hanging his

elbow out the window. He shifted in his seat, adding, "Feels good to have those stitches removed." He rubbed a place on his chest and said, "While they were taking things out, they put in a port for the chemo, you know. Alice says they'll want to start next week. She's setting up the appointments today."

"They won't do that here, will they?" Callie asked, backing the truck around and pulling out onto the street.

"No, no. We'll have to go to Oklahoma City. Didn't Rex explain?"

She shook her head. "No, he didn't."

"Well, you and Bodie won't mind taking a little trip, will you?"

Callie looked at him in surprise. "Bodie and I need to go?"

"I think you should," Wes said. "Otherwise, I'll worry about you. Rex agrees. He doesn't want Dolent pestering you while we're gone or your father pressuring you."

Sighing, Callie said, "I don't want to be a burden."

To her surprise, Wes said, "It's not about that, girl. I don't think I have to tell you that death changes those left behind. I've been lonely and filled with regret since Glory went to the Lord. She and I discussed it and decided that we wouldn't try to hold our kids to the ranch. I'm not so sure now that was the wise move, but Glory, she never doubted, and I miss that certainty—and everything else— about her. Now, Dr. Shorter, she's angry, and it keeps her from seeing the truth. Your father, well, he's never been the same since your mother died."

Callie couldn't have been more shocked. "You knew him well back then?"

"I did. We were good friends, Jane and Stu, me and Glory. He was a lot softer in those days, fun and relaxed, so in love with your mom and you. Her death broke him, frightened him, I think. He'd have wrapped you in cotton batting and locked you away to protect you, if he could have. He wasn't going to send you to public school. Did you know that?"

Gaping at him, Callie nearly ran a stop sign, braking only at the last moment. The truck rocked to a stop. She stared at Wes.

"I didn't."

"The pastor had to talk to him. He finally saw reason, but it wasn't easy for him. I think he shifted his focus to money because getting rich was the only way he could protect you and control your world."

"You try to let go of your children because you love them," Callie said, moving the truck forward again, "and my dad tries to hold on to me for the same reason."

Wes chuckled. "Hadn't thought of it that way, but you're right. Who's to say we aren't both wrong?"

"I don't know," Callie told him. "I just know I can't marry Ben Dolent."

Laughing, Wes shook his head. "No, you cannot, and if Stu was thinking straight, he'd know it, too. Until he gets his head right, I think you ought to tag along with us to Oklahoma City, though."

"We'll see," she said.

Rex and Meredith agreed with Wes and even argued that Callie could be quite useful in Oklahoma City. It was decided that Callie and Bodie would stay with Meredith in her apartment and Rex would stay in the hospital suite with Wes but take daily meals with Callie and Bodie at Meredith's place. Meredith would spend as much time with Wes as her nursing schedule would allow, and Callie should feel free to make herself at home in Meredith's apartment, using the washer and dryer as necessary and taking care of Meredith's two cats.

Callie pointed out that they were paying her rather well to basically babysit two cats, cook a few meals and do a couple loads of laundry.

Rex lifted his eyebrows and drawled, "You haven't seen Meredith's apartment."

Wes hid a smile behind his hand. "Let's just say that Meredith is an animal nut."

"More animal nut than housekeeper," Rex muttered.

Callie didn't have time to give that statement much thought. Over the ensuing week, Wes grew rapidly stronger and obviously put on weight. He seemed to be eating with that purpose in mind, and the supplements that Dr. Shorter had him on meant swallowing numerous pills before and after every meal. Callie kept busy keeping him fed, the house clean, the laundry done and Bodie halfway satisfied.

While Wes seemed to be gaining strength and pounds, Rex seemed to be losing both. He came in for lunch every day all but burned to a crisp by the June sun and nearly fell asleep in his plate at the dinner table every evening. At midday Saturday, however, he happily announced that the alfalfa had been completely baled.

"We can leave for Oklahoma City without any fear for the alfalfa, at least. Duffy and the boys will move it to storage while we're gone. Then I'll start on the regular hay when we get back."

"Good job, son," Wes told him. "The alfalfa fields would be going fallow if not for you."

"That's what I'm here for, Dad."

"Got a cold watermelon for lunch," Callie announced. "How does a peach cobbler sound with dinner?"

"Sounds great," Rex replied. "I want about a three-hour soak in the tub between meals, though. Then you'll probably need to clean the bathtub with a shovel."

Everyone laughed at that, including Bodie, who didn't have the foggiest idea what might be funny. She felt better, though, now that those two bottom teeth had finally broken through.

"Look at that!" Rex exclaimed, seeing her smile. "We have teeth."

"We do, indeed," Callie said, pulling down Bodie's chin to show off the new acquisitions. "Hopefully we'll have a better week. I was praying she'd get them in before we had to travel."

Wes shot a look at Rex, who smiled and nodded. "Glad she's feeling better."

"Me, too," Callie said, dropping a kiss onto Bodie's forehead and receiving another toothy grin in response. To her surprise, when Rex stood, Bodie reached for him.

"Is it okay?" he asked, stopping himself as he reached for the baby.

"Of course."

Smiling, he lifted the baby out of her chair and cuddled her against him, murmuring, "I'm too dirty for you, munchkin."

"She has to have a bath anyway," Callie said. "I'll bathe her in the sink after I clean up the lunch dishes."

"I used to take a bath in that sink," Rex told Bodie. "I wasn't as cute as you, though."

Callie chuckled and cleared the table while Bodie charmed Rex. Afterward, she bathed and packed suitcases for herself and Bodie before putting the baby down for her afternoon nap.

Rex waited until Sunday after church to pack for himself and Wes. They all turned in early on Sunday evening and woke well before dawn on Monday to breakfast of cinnamon rolls and fruit salad that Callie had made for them. Bodie wasn't happy about the early hour, but she soon slipped off to sleep again in her car seat.

They hit the tail end of the morning rush hour in the city, but Rex had experience driving in traffic and negotiated the many lanes of swiftly moving vehicles with ease. He took them straight to the cancer wing of the hospital. His sister Meredith waited for them, her long, straight, pale red hair parted on the side and framing her pretty face, vibrant blue eyes, pert nose and wide smile.

A cheerleader in high school, she'd lost none of her perkiness. She bounced over to Wes and threw her arms around him, then did the same with Rex and Callie, enveloping Bodie along with her.

"She's adorable, Callie, adorable."

"Thank you, but she's not so adorable when she's cutting teeth."

"You like kitties?" Meredith crooned, tickling Bodie under her chin. "I think my kitties will love you."

Rex made a snorting sound, which earned him a playful slap on the arm from his sister. Bodie looked at Callie as if to ask what was going on. Callie just shook her head. Bodie suddenly launched herself at Rex, who caught her just in time and clutched her against his chest. She stuck her hand in her mouth and almost casually swung a little foot at Meredith.

Wes chortled. "Better watch it, Meredith. Rex has a protector now."

"So I see."

Callie put her hand over her mouth, for it did seem that Bodie had sent a warning kick at Meredith, and it wouldn't do for her to see her mother grinning as if in approval. Both Rex and Meredith looked as tickled as Wes.

Reaching for her daughter, Callie said, "Come here, Miss Mess." To her surprise, Bodie turned away from her, looping an arm around Rex's neck.

"She's okay," Rex said, crooking his arm around her. He lifted his chin at Meredith, adding, "Besides, I might need her."

"You might," Meredith teased, but then she took her father's arm, saying, "Come on, Dad. Let's get you checked in."

Wes sighed. "If we have to, we have to."

Rex stayed behind with Callie and Bodie in the waiting area. Bodie stood between Rex's knees, bouncing up and down and gnawing on the seam of his jeans, making a big wet spot.

"Are you sure she's not bothering you?" Callie asked anxiously.

"She's fine. It's okay for her to get the denim in her mouth, though, right?"

"She's had worse in her mouth, trust me," Callie muttered.

Rex chuckled. "You're a great mother. Dad says you're far better with Bodie than my mama was with me."

That shocked Callie. "Really? I always thought Gloria was the perfect mom."

"She was great," Rex said, "but apparently

there was a learning curve." Callie felt her eyes fill with tears. "Hey," Rex said, reaching for her hand. "Even the best mama has to start at the beginning."

"That's just such a relief to hear," Callie told him, laughing and blinking away the moisture.

"Mama," Bodie said very clearly then.

Callie gasped. Reaching down, she swept Bodie up into her arms and began dancing her around the waiting area while Rex laughed and clapped his hands.

"Mama loves you," Callie whispered, coming to a stop in front of her chair again.

Rex stood and patted Bodie on the back, grinning. "What's not to love? We have here a beautiful baby girl with her first two teeth who can now say, 'Mama.' Sounds perfect to me."

"Mama!" Bodie exclaimed triumphantly, and Callie put her head back, laughing. Delighted, Bodie said it again, "Mama!"

"Well, she's got that down," Rex quipped. "We've got *hi*, *bye* and *mama*. What's next?"

Callie felt the joy drain out of her. For most children, next would naturally be *dada*, but not for Bodie. Sadly, not for her fatherless little girl. Callie shook her head.

"I don't know. It's probably my imagination, but sometimes I think she may be trying to say 'Night-night,' too."

"Nie-nie-nie," Bodie muttered, digging a finger into her mother's chin. She then laughed as if she'd done something very clever.

"Well done, Miss Bodie," Rex said, patting her again. "Very well done."

She suddenly made a grab for his ear with one hand and his neck with the other. Callie scolded her.

"Bodie! Stop."

Rex laughed, gathering her into his arms. "That's it, kiddo. Go where the compliments are." More, Callie thought, to disengage her hold on his ear than to thrill her, Rex dandled the baby over his head then had to dodge the drool that splattered his shoulder. "Ladylike little thing, aren't you," he quipped, bringing her down to rest in the crook of his arm.

Bodie promptly scrunched up her face and turned bright red.

"Uh-oh," Callie gasped. "I think a diaper change is in order."

Rex started to laugh. "You think?"

Callie took her daughter into her hands, careful to avoid her bottom, while both she and Rex laughed until tears ran down their faces.

Callie dipped down to snag her bag from its place on the floor beside her chair. "Want to learn how to change a diaper?" she teased.

"No." He shook his head.

"Coward."

"Yes." He nodded.

She looked around in search of the nearest ladies' room.

"Over there," he said, pointing. "Here, I'll show you."

Still grinning, he took the bag and led the way down a short hallway. Just as they reached the door, it opened and an older woman came out. Dressed in a neat gray suit near the same shade as her short, wispy hair and wire-framed glasses, she wore bright pink lipstick.

She took one look at the three of them and exclaimed, "Oh, what a pretty baby!"

"Thank you," Callie said, reaching for the bag that Rex passed to her.

"She has her mama's hair and eyes," the woman announced. Then she looked at Rex and added, "But I think she has her daddy's mouth."

"Oh, he's—" Callie began.

"She's much better looking than me," Rex said at the same time.

The woman started to giggle, and Callie muttered, "We need a clean diaper."

"Obviously," Rex added.

"Go see about Wes, please," Callie hissed around a smile.

He executed an about-face. "Going to see about Wes."

Bodie squeaked and reached for him, bucking in her mother's arms. "Not without a clean diaper, honey," Callie told her, exasperated by the child's sudden attachment to Rex.

The smiling woman adjusted her glasses and said, "He seems like a keeper."

Callie just nodded and pushed through the restroom door with her shoulder. He might well be a keeper, but she wouldn't be the one keeping him, no matter how irresistible he might seem or how fond of him her daughter might be.

She just hoped that Bodie wasn't growing too fond of Rex—or Wes, for that matter. As she cleaned Bodie and wrestled a new diaper onto her, Callie told herself that she had no reason to worry. Bodie wouldn't remember Rex and Wes after she and Callie had gone on to whatever place God had prepared for them.

No, the only heart Callie had to worry about becoming overly fond of the Billings men was her own.

Chapter Seven

"Wow."

Rex followed Callie's gaze as she trailed the colorful maze of tunnels, scratching posts and activity centers that filled the walls and much of the floor of the living room of the apartment, which was on the ground floor of the building.

"Dad did mention that my sister is an animal lover."

Callie grinned. "I think the word he used was *nut*."

Rex chuckled. "Well, Dad always did like to cut right to the heart of a matter."

"You're sure she only has two cats?" Callie asked worriedly, looking around again in awe.

"Just two," he confirmed, slipping past her with suitcases for her and Bodie. "That's all her lease allows." He pushed the door almost closed with his foot to keep the aforementioned cats from escaping their palace.

"All this for two cats," Callie said, shaking her head. Even Bodie seemed to be taking it all in from her perch on her mother's hip.

"The good news is that you'll hardly ever see them except at feeding time. The litter box is on the enclosed patio, and they have a pet door to let themselves in and out. The bad news is that all this doesn't leave much room for company, so the only TV is in her bedroom."

"Make yourself at home in there," Meredith said, pushing through the door behind them, grocery bags weighing down her arms. She kicked the door closed behind her. "I have a sitting area so feel free to go in and watch TV anytime you want. When I'm not sleeping or dressing, that is."

Rex rolled his eyes, and Callie laughed. "I don't need TV. I have a baby, plenty to read and meals to cook." She turned a circle, looking around her again, and asked, "When was the last time you dusted all this?"

"You don't want to know," Meredith answered, carrying the groceries through the dining area into the kitchen.

"Actually, I do," Callie refuted calmly. "I'm not sure how Bodie will react to cat dander."

"Ooh, I hadn't thought of that," Meredith admitted, looking around the end of the kitchen wall.

"I'll get the rest of the stuff out of the car," Rex said quickly.

As he went out the door, he heard Callie talking to Meredith about cleaning supplies. He'd thought he was being generous when he'd set her salary, but he really was not paying that woman enough. The last time he'd mentioned cat dander to his sister, she'd nearly taken his head off. Meredith kept a clean house—she was a nurse, after all—but she'd given over her whole living room and a large portion of her life to those cats. Maybe Callie could at least bring some perspective to the situation.

He carried in the remainder of the groceries and put Callie's and Bodie's bags in the extra bedroom, while Meredith and Callie laughed together in the kitchen and put away the groceries. Rex stood in the pathway between the dining area and the kitchen to ask where Callie wanted the portable crib.

"Feel free to move the furniture if you need to," Meredith told her, waving her into the other room. "You'll find a luggage stand in the closet."

Callie carried Bodie out of the kitchen, past

Rex and just down the hall to the small guest room, where a double bed and a long, low dresser took up most of the space.

"Well, I guess we should push the bed into the corner, slide over the nightstand and put the crib below the window in front of the one closet door. We can put the suitcases in the other end of the closet."

"Works for me."

"Need any help?"

"Naw, I got it."

"I'll go help Meredith then."

He nodded and started scooting the bed against the wall on one side. When he had the furniture positioned, he went back out to the truck and got the portable crib. Ten minutes after he had it set up, Callie disappeared into the bedroom and closed the door. Ten minutes after that, she remerged to say that Bodie was sleeping and that she would be starting lunch.

"What can I do?" Meredith asked.

"Don't you have to work later?"

"Not for a few hours."

"I'm guessing that means you got up early after working late to meet us and check your dad into the chemo unit," Callie said.

"Well, yeah, of course."

"Go sit with your brother," Callie directed. "After lunch, you can take a nap."

Meredith looked at Rex. "Dad's right. She's pure gold."

Callie laughed. "I don't know if Billings' standards are just low or if you've all simply had to do for yourselves too long. Either way, thank you. Now, go away and let me work while my baby is sleeping."

"You don't have to tell me twice," Rex said, turning down the hallway toward his sister's room. Meredith followed, but by the time they reached her room, both cats had joined them, appearing seemingly out of nowhere.

Tux, the black-and-white tom, hopped up onto the love seat while Tiger, the yellow-striped fellow, paced back and forth in front of the armchair, as if to say that Rex must not sit until their mistress had chosen her spot. She took the love seat, and both cats claimed space around her. The bed sat on a raised platform behind them, while the television hung over the dresser in front of them.

"Talked to Ann lately?" he asked conversationally. Their sister rarely contacted him, but to be fair, he wasn't very good about staying in touch with either of his sisters.

Meredith nodded. "She called last night to ask what I think Dad's chances are."

"Of beating the cancer, you mean."

"Yes."

Rex tried not to ask, but he couldn't help himself. "So what *do* you think his chances are?"

Meredith petted her cats, one with each hand. "Better than fifty-fifty, I'd say."

Only better than fifty-fifty? Rex felt as if a fist closed around his heart. "I thought, because they didn't find it in his pancreas..."

"It's tricky," she told him softly. "Besides the liver, every one of the lymph nodes that they took was positive for cancer."

Rex sighed and pushed both hands through his hair. "No wonder they insisted on starting the chemo so soon after surgery."

"I wish it could've waited a few weeks," Meredith said. "My leave still hasn't come through, and I'm not sure it will until the next hiring rotation."

"We'll manage," Rex assured her. "You'll run interference for us this week, and Callie will be there when we go home."

"I'm so thankful you have her because you're going to need her," Meredith warned.

Rex nodded and tried to focus on more pleasant subjects, such as how much of the cat paradise in the front room Meredith intended to move to the Straight Arrow with her. They were arguing good-naturedly about where she could build her cat playground at the ranch when Callie came to tell them that lunch was ready. The three of them sat down to a light meal and casual conversation.

It was the last truly easy moment of the week. Rex didn't expect the accommodations at the hospital to be hotel quality, and he was tired enough to sleep well the first night. But the reality of his father's disease made itself felt in a new way repeatedly throughout every day. Even as they steadily pumped the chemotherapy drugs into his body, one specialist after another came to Wes's room, including a dietician, who asked to speak to Callie after learning they had a cook. They arranged the meeting, and Rex went down to the common area to play with Bodie while Callie met with the dietician.

He hadn't realized that babies could be so engaging. Bodie, of course, was incredibly bright; she was much brighter than the average child, he felt sure. She mimicked his facial expressions, laughed when he made funny sounds and gave slimy, messy kisses that completely melted his heart even as they turned his stomach a little. Fear tainted every moment, however. What if he dropped her or scared her? What if she filled another diaper before her mother returned to deal with it? What if she started to cry?

His relief warred with his disappointment

when Callie finally returned. Then Bodie both thrilled him and broke his heart when she tried to hang on to him rather than go to her mother.

"Bodie Jane Deviner, behave yourself," Callie scolded, pulling the child away from Rex. Bodie huffed such a pathetically false wail of protest that even Rex knew she wasn't really crying. Callie had to disguise a smile of her own in order to deal with the babe. "That's enough now."

Bodie rubbed her eyes with both fists, showing the true source of her distress. She obviously knew that if she went with her mom, at some point she'd have to take a nap. No doubt that apartment seemed pretty small to the two of them by now, and Bodie was too young for the playground in Meredith's complex.

"There's a park we could take her to after dinner, if you're interested," Rex heard himself say.

Callie smiled. "That might be a good idea if it's shady enough."

"I think it is."

"Okay, but first someone needs a n-a-p."

He chuckled. "We're spelling now, are we?"

"Oh, yes."

Definitely brighter than average, and a bright spot in an otherwise dark week. Just like her mom.

* * *

The heat felt absolutely suffocating, even after dinner, but just seeing something green made Callie feel better.

"Why is the city so much hotter than the country?" she asked, lowering her body gratefully onto a bench in the shade of a well-groomed tree.

"I don't know. It's a different kind of heat, isn't it?" Rex replied, wiping his forehead on his sleeve. "I guess it's all the concrete, metal and glass."

Callie fluffed her bangs off her damp forehead, grumbling, "I don't understand why anyone lives here."

He spread his hands. "Shopping, entertainment, beautiful homes, state-of-the-art hospitals, jobs, friends, family, schools, libraries, museums, sports. Cities do have their advantages."

"I guess. I just know I'll be glad to get home again."

"Me, too."

That surprised her, and she couldn't help staring at him. "I thought you'd be reluctant to leave city living behind."

He shook his head. "Not this time. I'm sick to death of all the needles and pills and monitors. I don't want to see another doctor or technician for years. And I want my father back."

"Meredith says it's going to get worse before it gets better," Callie warned.

Rex sighed. "I know. We'll have to do this again in a few weeks."

"What happens if he doesn't make it, Rex?" Callie asked gently.

He shrugged, then ran his hands through his hair. "The same thing that happens if he does. Eventually, one way or another, we all go on with our lives. Meri goes on nursing. Ann keeps climbing the corporate ladder. I go back to practicing law. What other choice is there?"

Callie didn't like to admit, even to herself, how bitterly she felt the disappointment that swept through her. She hadn't even realized until that very moment that some secret part of her had hoped he would say that he'd stay on at the Straight Arrow and make it his own. She hadn't wanted to admit, even to herself, that on some level she'd been hoping to make it her own, too. Somehow, in a very short time, the Straight Arrow had become more than a job to her; it had truly become *home*.

These last few days, staying at Meredith's apartment, Callie had come to understand that such accommodations were the best that she and Bodie could hope for on their own in the future. It was fine, better than the rough cabin at the campground that she and Bo had enjoyed as newlyweds, but not the spacious, comfortable, somehow more meaningful place that the Billings' ranch house represented. That wasn't really why she'd hoped to stay, however.

Wes and Rex had become like family to her, not to mention to her daughter, who crawled into Rex's lap at the first opportunity. He made funny noises and faces to entertain her. Bodie giggled, her eyes dancing. Not satisfied with that, Rex blew raspberries against her cheeks until she squealed with laughter. With her little belly shaking, Bodie turned red in the face with her glee, while her mother sat there silently grieving the loss of something she'd never had, a partner in parenting, a home at the ranch.

It was insanity. She and Rex were not a couple, and he hadn't given her the slightest hint that they could be. Besides, she'd always intended to leave the Straight Arrow. Yet, suddenly, all she could think about was who would take care of Wes after she'd gone? And who would take care of Rex when he went back to his other life? Some as yet faceless, nameless woman would surely step into the latter role. Callie didn't want to know or hear about her, which just proved that she was even more foolish than her baby girl.

"You know, I think it's too hot out here for her," Callie suddenly announced, placing her hands over Bodie's red cheeks.

"Sure," Rex said, rising at once to his feet, but when Callie reached for her daughter, he was already turning down the path, a happy Bodie riding in the crook of his arm. They looked so much like father and daughter.

Why hadn't he told that woman at the hospital that he wasn't Bodie's father? Maybe he'd thought it would be less embarrassing. Callie refused to think it was anything else. After all, not even sixteen months had passed since her husband had died.

That was almost three times longer than they'd been married.

Such thoughts seemed traitorous and sent her into silent prayer.

Lord, take control of my thoughts and desires, guide me and help me stay in Your will. Make me want what You want for me.

Suddenly, Rex spun in a circle, the baby safely clasped against his chest. Bodie's laughter called a smile from Callie and sent her prayers onto a new trail.

Thank You for the Billings family and all they've come to mean to us. Make Bodie and

*me blessings to them. Please heal Wes and re-
turn him to the Straight Arrow, and give them
all the desires of their hearts, for all the good
that they have done us...*

She felt steadier by the time they got back to
the apartment. Rex didn't come in because he
wanted to get back to his father. Bodie tried her
new clingy act, holding on to Rex and huffing
piteously, but her attention shifted the instant
Callie mentioned "kitties."

Though the cats had wisely avoided Bodie's
grasp, darting in and out of her proximity just
enough to tantalize her and guarantee her interest, Bodie had developed an intense curiosity about the animals. She even tried to call
them, clicking her tongue and squealing inco-
herently at them. Confident that the cats would
keep their distance, Callie had allowed her
to try to entice them. She'd even allowed her to
safely pet them when Meredith was around to
hold them. Watching them running through
their indoor playground had entertained Bodie
for hours, while Callie lay on the floor with
her, reading.

As for Callie, she welcomed the more pro-
ductive pastimes of cooking and cleaning.
Thankfully, she had to endure only one more
day before she could pack their bags, collapse

the portable crib and move the furniture back into its customary place.

On the day of departure, Wes arrived at Meredith's apartment on Rex's arm, a bag of freshly filled prescriptions in hand and a wan smile in place. He looked a little grayer to Callie but seemed in good spirits, despite the surgical mask that the doctors had insisted he wear until he got home. It didn't last that long as the jostling of the pickup seemed to upset his stomach.

Soon, they arrived back at the house to find Duffy waiting.

He helped get Wes into the house and the truck unloaded. Then he stepped aside with Rex.

"It's Soldier," Callie heard him say, referring to Wes's beloved stud. "He somehow cut a foreleg. We called the vet. He put in some stitches and applied a dressing. Now it's wait and see."

Rex sighed. "Thanks, Duff. I'll phone Dr. Burns and check on the horse myself later. Tomorrow we need to get back into the field. Make sure Woody and Cam are ready for an early start, will you?"

"Yes, sir."

Obviously, Rex intended to waste no time getting back to work. While Rex talked to his dad about the horse, Callie prepared a light supper in keeping with the dietician's suggestions. Wes ate in his room, too tired and ill to come to the table. When Callie went in to pick up his dishes, he was talking to Ann on the phone, trying to sound jolly and reassuring.

"I'm fine, sugar. Don't worry about me. Rex and Callie are taking good care of me. Your sister's a nurse. She sees too much, and it concerns her. You need to help her keep her spirits up."

Callie wanted to hug him and tell him what a good father he was. Even now, as he fought for his life, his concern for his children could not have been more evident. She couldn't help envying his daughters and wishing that she had the kind of relationship with her dad that Meredith and Ann had with Wes.

He soon drifted off to sleep under the influence of the antinausea drugs. Rex couldn't seem to relax, however, and checked on his dad repeatedly throughout the evening. He pretended to watch television, but Callie could see that he was poised to go to his father at any moment, attuned to signals of distress from the back of the house. She doubted he would rest at all that night.

"I have something that might help," she said when he returned from another one of his quiet trips to Wes's room. "Wait here." Rising from her seat on the sofa, she quickly padded up the stairs and slipped into the room that she shared with her daughter.

Bodie slept on her side, making sweet little breathing sounds. Callie smiled and tiptoed across the room to the nightstand. Carefully, she opened the drawer and removed the baby monitor set that she'd stored there. She'd received it as a gift but had barely used it. She and Bodie had always lived in very close quarters, either in the same room or right next door to each other. When she'd come here, she'd thought she might use it for Bodie's afternoon naps, but she'd forgotten about it, and her daughter didn't have any trouble making herself heard when she woke and wanted attention.

Quietly, Callie slipped out of the room again and carried the box with the baby monitor and receiver downstairs. She handed it to Rex, who had resumed his seat in the recliner.

"Put the main unit in your dad's room, and keep the receiver in your room or with you when you're around the house. That way, if he wakes ill during the night, you'll hear him."

Rex looked up at her. "But don't you need this?"

She shook her head. "Not really. Mrs. Lightner used it a few times, but somehow I just…" She shook her head again.

"You always know when she needs you, don't you?" he asked, smiling. "I've seen it. You hear her before anyone else does. It's almost as if you hear her before she cries."

Callie shrugged. "Just use it. You might sleep better tonight if you do."

Rex nodded and started getting up. "You're right."

He carried the set into the kitchen, where he unboxed it on the table and turned it on, making sure the batteries were still good. Then he took the monitor into his father's room, returning a few moments later to pick up the small receiver and carry it back into the living room.

"Thank you," he told her, carefully tuning the thing. Wes's soft snore and the rustle of bedclothes transmitted clearly. Rex looked up, and his blue gaze seemed charged with something more than gratitude, but Callie knew she'd be insane even to think about it.

"I think I'll turn in," she quickly decided, hopping to her feet.

He looked away then, lightly replying, "I'm going to sit down, rewind this program and actually watch it now."

She chuckled, nodded and turned toward the stairs again. "Good night."

"Good night, Callie. Will you pray for my dad tonight?"

"I will," she promised. "You, too."

"Thank you," he said again with such feeling this time that she gave in to a very foolish impulse. Zipping across the room, she hugged him.

She didn't know why she did it. He'd just seemed so needy and worried, so alone in that moment. She'd wanted to help.

He wrapped his long, strong arms around her and laid his cheek against the crown of her head. After a long, tender moment, he pulled in a deep breath and straightened. Callie stepped back.

Gently tucking her hair behind her ears with both hands, he smiled. "I needed that. Seems you always know just how to help."

Smiling and shaking her head, she moved back toward the stairs. "Sleep well."

He picked up the receiver to the baby monitor and saluted her with it. "I will."

Hurrying away, she began to fear that she'd always want to help Rex Billings.

Chapter Eight

Wes slept well, and because Wes slept well, Rex rested well enough to start the day early the next morning. He hadn't shared his plans with Callie because he didn't think it fair to ask her to rise before dawn when he knew that she was going to have her hands full with his dad and Bodie. Creeping past her door with his boots in hand and his hat perched on the back of his head, he tiptoed down the stairs, only to find the light on in the kitchen and a box waiting for him on the landing.

He sat down on the steps and pulled on his boots, then settled his hat and investigated the box, finding two large bottles of sports drink, a thermos of coffee, a fat breakfast sandwich and a bunch of grapes. Popping a grape into his mouth, he started down the steps to the kitchen, only to freeze when he heard a thin wail from above.

Callie immediately appeared, clad in a floral print cotton robe, her feet bare. She smiled as she ran lightly up the steps. Fearing that any conversation on the stairs would wake his father, he stepped back to allow her to pass, then followed. Callie entered her bedroom, leaving the door open, and plucked the fussing baby from her low crib. Bodie rubbed her eyes sleepily and dropped her head onto her mom's shoulder. Callie turned back to the door. Rex braced his forearms against the frame and smiled apologetically.

"Sorry if I got you guys up early," he said softly. "Wasn't my intention."

"I know. I heard you talking with Duffy yesterday." She kept her voice low, patting Bodie on the back as she swayed side to side.

He hung his head, bowled over by Callie's kindness. "You take on too much. I wanted to let you sleep in this morning."

"That's not necessary," she told him, carefully laying Bodie down on the foot of her bed to change a soggy diaper.

"Will she go back to sleep?" he asked softly.

"I think so," Callie said as she worked. "I'll nurse her and put her down again."

"I've hired some extra help," he told her for

some reason, watching her pick up the baby again, "all I could find, so I need to get out there." He was painfully aware that he was stalling, enjoying the sweetness of these quiet predawn moments.

Callie picked up Bodie and rose. Bodie rubbed her eyes again then reached for him. It was if she reached into his chest and squeezed his heart with that grasping little hand. He didn't have time to hold and play with her, but he caught her hand and kissed her tiny fingers, carefully because he hadn't shaved. Her bright baby smile induced him to step closer and kiss her soft, plump cheek. Wrinkling her button nose, she giggled. Callie laughed softly. Before he could even think, he turned his head and kissed Callie's cheek, too.

Both shocked, they stared at each other with wide, stunned eyes before his brain finally kicked into gear.

He blurted out, "I don't know why I did that. But, um, thanks, and…" He blinked before he could think what else he needed to say. "Gotta go."

"See you for lunch," she whispered, ducking her head.

Nodding, he quickly left, snatching up the box on his way. That woman would make someone an ideal wife. Some rancher, which he was *not*.

If he'd had any doubt about that, the idea was reinforced when roughly half of his expected extra help failed to show up by the appointed time.

A teenager named Jock Aster apologized for his father's absence, telling Rex, "Dad meant to be here, Mr. Billings, but he had to work for Mr. Crowsen instead. He asked me to apologize for him. The thing is, we owe Crowsen a pretty big feed bill, and we can't afford to be cut off."

Rex couldn't quite believe that Crowsen would go so far as to punish Rex and Wes for hiring Callie by applying pressure to anyone else who might work for the Straight Arrow. That being the case, however, then Aster was to be commended for not keeping his son at home, too.

"It's okay, Jock," Rex told the boy. "We'll manage." But not having the crew he'd counted on complicated matters substantially.

Any doubts Rex had about the reasons for the situation vanished when he stepped up onto the porch at lunchtime and found young A. G. Carruthers waiting there. Tall, thin A.G. had been hired to drive his flatbed truck through the field so the stackers could toss the bales onto it for transport to the various storage barns throughout the property. When A.G. hadn't shown up, their transportation had been cut in half, which had lengthened the hay harvest time by at least four days, so Rex was glad to see him, until A.G. explained that he couldn't come to work for the Straight Arrow.

"I thought I owed you a personal explanation," A.G. said, turning his billed cap in his hands.

"Let me guess," Rex ventured. "Stuart Crowsen."

A.G. nodded, his prominent Adam's apple bobbing as he gulped. "When my dad died last year, we didn't have a penny to bury him. I went down to the bank for a loan. Crowsen offered a personal loan instead, with my place as collateral. It was just six thousand dollars, with variable payments, which made it sound easy, but I didn't read the fine print well enough. Every time I'm a dollar short or a day late, Crowsen jacks up the interest. I owe more on it now than I did when I started, and if it's not paid by a certain date, he can make a claim on my place. I don't dare go against him."

"That sounds downright usurious," Rex mused, rubbing his prickly chin.

"I don't know about that," A.G. said. "He

keeps offering to buy my place, and it's a fair offer, but I don't want to sell."

"Have you got a copy of those loan papers?"

"I do, and every letter I've had from him since I borrowed that money."

"I'd like to see them, if you don't mind."

A.G. looked taken aback. "Well...what for?"

"Legal curiosity," Rex replied lightly. "Haven't had my lawyer hat on in a while. Can't hurt to take a look, can it?"

Frowning, A.G. seemed to think that over. "Guess not."

"But let's keep it just between us for now. Okay?"

That seemed to reassure the younger man. "Okay. I'll bring 'em by later."

"Good enough. Now, my lunch is waiting for me, and since Callie Deviner is a fine cook, I'm anxious for it."

A speculative look entered A.G.'s pale gray eyes. "Is that so?" He ran a bony hand through his dishwater-blond hair. "Knew she was a looker. Didn't know she was a cook, too."

Rex half expected him to shine his boots on the legs of his jeans and ask to speak to her. He'd completely forgotten that A.G. was single, and around here Stuart Crowsen's daughter would be considered quite a catch, especially as she was completely lovely and sweet. Irritated with himself as much as A.G., Rex told himself to keep his big mouth shut where Callie was concerned. And his thoughts elsewhere.

"I'd invite you in," he explained, "but Dad can't have company because of his chemo."

"Oh, no, I know. Callie explained it to me when I first got here. You tell Mr. Wes that Mom and me are praying for him."

"Thank you. I will."

The two men shook hands before A.G. departed. Rex went inside and straight to the small bathroom beneath the stairs to wash up before presenting himself in the kitchen. Callie had hung a clean shirt on a hook inside the door, so he stripped to the waist and put it on. Wes was not at the table, but Bodie played happily in the old playpen. She pulled up to one knee, lifting her arms. How could he resist that? He picked her up and clasped her lightly to his chest.

"Hey, sugar. What are you doing up? Isn't this usually your nap time?"

She planted a sloppy, openmouthed kiss right over the end of his nose that made him laugh and wipe his face.

"Yes, this is usually her nap time," Callie said, carrying a plate to the table before taking Bodie from his arms, "but she slept later than usual this morning."

"My fault. Sorry."

Callie shook her head. "No one's fault. Sit down and eat."

He straddled the chair and sat. "How's Dad?"

Callie shook her head again. "Tough morning."

Rex sighed. "What can I do?"

"You're doing it. He just needs to know that the hay harvest is going well."

"It's going fine," Rex said, focusing on his plate. Slower than he'd like, but that was nothing to worry about. So long as it didn't rain.

"Did you speak to A.G.?"

"Yep. He'll be back later with some papers for me. If I'm not here, just put them on the desk in the study."

"Okay."

Rex ate quickly, then rose and prepared to go to his father's room.

"He's sleeping," Callie warned, placing a plastic jug of iced tea on the table, along with a trio of energy bars, "but I'll tell him that you looked in." Rex nodded and stuffed the energy bars into his shirt pocket. "And if you want, you can take your dinner in his room with him tonight. I don't think he'll feel up to the table for a while."

Rex felt a pang of disappointment, but he said, "That'll be good."

"I think Wes will like it," Callie told him, smiling.

Returning her smile, Rex took the jug by the handle and walked off in the direction of his father's room. The door stood open, and Rex stopped there to look inside. As Callie had predicted, Wes slept heavily.

Something about him seemed different. Rex felt Callie at his elbow, and as if she'd read his mind, she whispered, "He asked me to cut his hair."

"I hadn't realized how gray he's gone," Rex said softly.

He felt her hand settle between his shoulder blades, a light, warm, comforting weight. After a moment, Rex turned away from his father's room and walked back down the hall past the kitchen, aware that Callie quietly, slowly followed, Bodie on her hip. Just before he stepped around the newel post at the end of the staircase into the foyer, he paused and looked back.

Callie lifted her free hand in a little gesture of farewell. Suddenly, Rex couldn't leave it just at that. This woman cooked his meals, did his laundry, took care of his ailing father, made their home. Yes, they paid her, but she did so much more than what they'd hired her to do.

He couldn't imagine doing this without her or that little bundle of joy on her hip.

He walked straight back down that hall and kissed Bodie in the center of her forehead, winning a toothy grin for his trouble. Then he kissed Callie in the center of her forehead, bangs and all. Grinning, he swept them a bow as he turned and headed for the door again, swinging the jug of tea and saying, "Later, my ladies."

Bodie babbled something he couldn't make out. Callie said not a word. It didn't matter. Rex was busy telling himself that kisses weren't necessarily romantic. In this case, it was more about gratitude than anything else.

And I am a lousy liar, Rex thought. *Even if I'm only trying to lie to myself. I'm going to dream about her again tonight. What an idiot I am. God help me.*

He meant it very sincerely. He very much needed some kind of intervention here. Callie was no more meant for him than the Straight Arrow was. When he'd graduated high school, he hadn't been able to get out of town fast enough. He'd gone off to college with bountiful eagerness, certain that he'd never want to return permanently, and he hadn't.

Tulsa had worked out well for him, at least until the implosion of his marriage. A graceful city with just enough money and society to provide a cosmopolitan atmosphere and a touch of culture, it was neither as large nor as frenetic as the state capitol, but it had suited him. He enjoyed a good workout at the gym and an occasional game of tennis, and until his divorce he'd been able to keep a horse and ride, not as often as he'd have liked, true, but he'd still enjoyed it.

After he'd left his job, he'd sent the horse, Diamond, a showy bay gelding, back here to the ranch. Then suddenly, his dad was fighting cancer and facing surgery, and Rex found himself following Diamond back to the Straight Arrow. That didn't mean either of them would be staying.

He had a law practice and a whole other life to get back to; until then, though, he had a job to do here. That hay wasn't going to bale, transport and store itself.

He climbed back into the truck and headed out to the field, tea and energy bars in tow.

Crowsen hadn't even bothered to have an attorney draw up the contract. He couldn't have. Even the worst attorney would have known that at least one of the provisions of his loan to A. G. Carruthers was illegal, but then a banker would have known that, too. Rex took no satisfaction in recommending that A.G. seek legal redress. In an effort to keep his name out of it, he declined to handle the case himself. The last thing he needed was more trouble with Stuart Crowsen. Instead, he sent A.G. to a friend of his in Healdton.

Tom Jackson was a fine lawyer, especially in a courtroom, but he had no taste for city life. He'd left a promising career in Tulsa for a general practice in his hometown. His own father was a banker, so he seemed a perfect choice to handle A.G.'s case. In only a matter of days, Tom called to thank Rex for the referral. He was too professional to discuss the merits of the case, but a week hadn't passed when A.G. reported that Crowsen had amended the terms of the loan, which A.G. had already paid off.

Nobody's fool, Crowsen had to know that he didn't have a legal leg to stand on, so he hadn't fought. Instead, he'd tried to quietly put the matter to rest, assuming that A.G.'s dependence on the Feed and Grain would keep the younger man quiet. A.G. was perhaps not as wise as he should have been, though, and he bragged about his victory. Soon, Rex had a steady stream of folks trekking out to the ranch with various loan papers and contracts in tow.

Most of the agreements that Rex reviewed were completely legal if somewhat, in Rex's personal opinion, unethical. Being the only source of money in town, Crowsen seemed to charge higher interest and exact stricter terms than most lenders. Rex repeatedly pointed out that it might be worth driving out of town to borrow.

In some instances, usually those involving smaller amounts and emergency situations, Stuart's terms were downright appalling. Rex sent those clients straight to Jackson, so many—seven in only days—that Tom referred several of them to other attorneys willing to take on Crowsen. It wouldn't take Stuart long to realize who was at the bottom of his troubles, so Rex reluctantly girded himself for a confrontation.

Meanwhile, Wes finally began to rally from his first chemotherapy treatment. Though company still wasn't recommended, he got out of the bed and came to the table for meals again. Over the course of the next ten days, the winter hay was finally baled. With the weatherman promising rain by the following Thursday, Rex took just enough of a break on Sunday for church before heading back into the field.

Now, with the remaining crew transporting and storing the fodder, Rex felt comfortable stealing Callie away for a couple hours. She'd worked as hard as he had. The hay had to be safely stored *today*, so Rex had even lent his, or rather, the ranch pickup to the task. He meant to ride horseback between the storage barns to make sure everything was in place and secured. With Soldier on the mend, Rex judged it an excellent time to give the old stud some much-needed exercise, and with Wes finally feeling better, Rex didn't see why Callie and Bodie couldn't accompany him and give Diamond a workout, too.

Even as he questioned the wisdom of having Callie to himself for a while, Rex couldn't deny the urge to spend some personal time with her. Besides, Bodie would be with them. She'd be as good a chaperone as they were likely to find. Now all he had to do was convince Callie.

"You ride, don't you?" he asked at the lunch table that Wednesday after Duffy had dropped him off at the house.

"Sure. Can't live around War Bonnet and not wind up on a horse at some time or other."

Rex glanced at his father, picked up the second half of his sandwich and said, "Well, then, what's the problem? I have two horses that need exercise, a crew that needs checking on, and just one me, unless you come along."

"What about Bodie?" she asked, as he'd known she would.

"My mom used to tie me to her waist and ride with me in front of her. Isn't that right, Dad?"

Wes smiled as if remembering. "That's right." He waved a hand at Bodie, adding, "You used to try to hold the reins even before you were her age." He shook his head, and Rex noticed that his hair was thinning. "Of course," Wes said, "that was before kids had to wear helmets just to ride bicycles."

"Helmet," Callie echoed, her big green eyes widening. "I should've thought of that. I hope it fits." She rubbed Bodie's head. "Wait here." With that, she ran from the room.

Rex looked at Wes, who shrugged, then at Bodie, who gave him a flirty grin, showing him her teeth. By the time Callie returned, Rex had polished off the rest of his sandwich and nearly everything else on the table. She had in hand a small silver helmet and a bright yellow plastic square.

"Bo and I used to ride our bicycles all over the campground. As soon as I told him I was pregnant, he bought this so we could take the baby with us one day. It was the smallest one he could find." She set it on Bodie's head. Bodie tilted her head back, looking up into the helmet. Everyone laughed, which only encouraged Bodie to try that again. Eventually, however, Callie got the chinstrap buckled. "It's still a little large, but I think it'll do."

"What is that other thing?" Wes asked.

"Oh. Well, I bought that," Callie said. "Living at the falls, I figured we'd have to take the baby swimming, so…" She unfolded the plastic square, revealing that it was actually a flotation vest.

After inflating the thing, they all realized that the helmet had to be removed so the vest could be slipped over Bodie's head. Callie belted the vest in place then went through the process of buckling the helmet again. Bodie wasn't happy with her strange new outfit, plucking and tugging at it, but the helmet and vest, which protected her front and back, would cushion her if she should fall from the horse. She'd be as safe as they could make her. Rex held her and laughed as she squirmed while her mom covered her arms and face with sunscreen. Then Callie packed up a small bag of necessities and another of drinks and snacks, and they were off, Rex admonishing Wes to call his cell phone if he had the slightest need.

"Don't worry about me," Wes said, waving them toward the door. "I'm gonna watch a little TV and take a nap."

"We won't be gone long," Rex promised. "Couple hours, tops."

"Take your time," Wes insisted. "Callie's already got dinner in the slow cooker. Everything else can wait."

Callie kissed the top of his head before carrying Bodie from the room. Rex noted the pleased, almost conspiratorial gleam in his father's eyes. Unless he missed his guess, the old man was indulging in a bit of matchmaking. Rex wished he could be wise enough *not* to enjoy it, but he had every intention of enjoying his time with Callie and Bodie, too.

What was not to enjoy, after all? A beautiful woman, a cute kid who adored him, a good horse and time to kill on a glorious day. It occurred to him as he saddled the horses and listened to Callie and Bodie making friends with them that on a day like today he'd probably have hit the gym, trying to make up for all the days he'd missed. Then he'd have cleaned up and looked for someone to share a meal with him. Afterward, he'd have gone back to his empty condo alone and listened to the TV while he worked on some case file or slipped off to sleep on the sofa while trying to read.

Rex had to shake his head when he thought of all the good that lifetime gym membership had done him. A few weeks on the ranch had accomplished more for his general fitness than all the workouts he'd forced himself to endure.

Come to think of it, his mood seemed lighter lately, despite his dad's medical condition. Must have something to do with all this sunshine. Didn't hurt that lately he'd felt a real sense of purpose, either.

The law mattered; he knew that, believed it. Somehow, though, the bigger the case the less it seemed to actually impact real people. He'd felt more satisfaction telling A. G. Carruthers to sue Stuart Crowsen for a few thousand bucks than he'd ever felt negotiating multimillion-dollar settlements between corporations, just as he'd felt more satisfaction sitting down at Callie's table than he had dining at the most sophisticated restaurants in Tulsa. A.G. was real people; Callie's food was real food.

Maybe ranch life was real life, and he'd just been too blind to see it until now.

He looked at Callie Deviner and her precious little daughter.

He wasn't blind anymore.

Chapter Nine

Rex's Diamond lived up to his name. Callie couldn't help admiring the animal. His black mane, tail and four black stockings set off a deep red coat relieved only by a small, white, diamond-shaped blaze on the forehead. His prancing gait proudly proclaimed that he knew he was beautiful, but he was just as beautifully behaved. The butternut sorrel stud by which Wes set such store, aptly named Soldier, was a taller, heavier horse, but age had mellowed his disposition. Unfortunately, Bodie literally screamed to go with Rex, holding out her arms and opening and closing her fingers in a grasping motion. Rex good-naturedly consented to parking her in front of him and allowing Callie to tie them together with the paisley shawl she'd brought for that purpose.

"This is ridiculous," she muttered to her

daughter as she knotted the cloth. "How did you get so spoiled?" Bodie just kicked a foot complacently and rammed her fingers in her mouth, the chinstrap on her helmet being too restrictive to allow her to get her fist in. Rex snickered, and Callie sent him a quelling glance. "You're not helping."

"Is it my fault if I'm irresistible?"

Callie rolled her eyes and went to mount her own horse. If he'd had any real idea how truly irresistible he was, she'd be in deep trouble. Bodie squealed with delight as they started off. Leaning forward, she grasped the saddle horn with both hands and tried to shake it. Rex kept an arm wrapped around her. She bucked and kicked and waved her hands, either trying to hurry things along or just enjoying herself. Then suddenly, several minutes into their ride, she seemed to look down and realize how far from the ground she sat.

Her little eyes went wide, and she fell back against Rex's chest with such force that he grunted. Her tiny fingers dug into his forearm.

"Ow. Her fingernails are sharp."

"Stop. She's scared."

He immediately brought the horse to a halt. Callie rode the bay up close to them and reached over to pat her daughter on the knee. Earlier, when Rex had donned a rather battered

straw cowboy hat, he'd offered Callie an old
baseball cap, which she now wore with sunglasses, her chin-length hair tucked behind her
ears. She wanted to tell him just how well he
wore his hat, but she didn't dare. Instead, she
pushed back the cap and shifted the glasses to
the brim before addressing her daughter.

"It's okay, baby. Mama's here. It's okay."

She caught Bodie by the hand and started
her horse slowly forward, Rex nudging his
mount along with hers. Soon Bodie relaxed.
Before long, she was kicking and squirming
and grasping the saddle horn again. They rode
to the first barn and found it tightly packed.
Rex told her that the seasoned hay had been
shifted to the front and the new cutting was
stored in the back. They dismounted there and
sat in the shade of a tree, sharing drinks and
conversation.

"So how do you really think Dad's doing?"
Rex asked after a few minutes.

"As well as can be expected," Callie answered honestly. "It's tough, but he's handling
it with as much grace as anyone could."

"I worry his pride will keep him from asking for help when he needs it."

"It may keep him from asking, but it doesn't
keep him from accepting help when it's offered."

"I guess that's good."

Callie nodded. "I think so."

"Well, I don't want to keep you away from him for too long," Rex said, clapping his hands against his thighs, "so I guess we should mount up."

This time, Bodie didn't protest when Callie took her onto the sorrel with her. Rex helped by continually engaging Bodie with smiles and funny noises. She liked that she could see herself in his mirrored sunglasses. They reached the second pole barn to find the men standing around scratching their heads, their trucks still filled with hay bales.

"What's going on?" Rex asked, leaning a forearm against his saddle horn.

Woody, the grizzled older hand, shifted a wad of tobacco from one side of his lower lip to the other with the tip of his tongue and said, "We've crammed hay into ever' nook and cranny we can find, boss, and now what're we s'posed to do?"

"Third barn's full?" Rex asked.

"I'm thinkin' we lifted her off the ground we stuffed so much under that metal roof."

"A good harvest then," Callie noted, smiling.

Rex calmly removed his sunglasses and pushed back his hat with his forearm. "I guess the rest of this better store up at the house barn then. Just remember not to feed it to the horses until it's aged. And ask Cam to check on Dad for me."

"Yes, sir, boss," Woody said, already turning away. He waved a hand over his head, shouting, "Y'all head to the house. I'll show you where to put it." Spitting a brown stream, he looked back over his shoulder at Rex. "I used to wipe your nose," he said, "*and* I shined your britches a time or two."

"Only when I deserved it," Rex admitted good-naturedly.

Woody grinned, showing teeth stained by the tobacco he used. "The old man's gonna be right pleased."

Rex smiled. "Still have the oats and sorghum to get in. Dean Pryor will be here to get that started before long."

"Yep." Woody squinted up at him. "Dean Paul Pryor's a good cutter. But there's the planting to start, you know. The late sorghum goes into the ground now, and the rye sows in early September, the barley just after. Then there's the late alfalfa harvest."

"We'll let Dad handle the rye and barley and what comes after," Rex decreed, gathering his reins up short.

"If you say so."

"That's how it has to be," Rex stated flatly. He couldn't have been clearer. He wouldn't even entertain the idea that Wes might not be well enough to handle the fall calendar, and he had no intention of staying on the Straight Arrow past the end of summer. Callie didn't know why that message pierced her; she'd known all along that Rex didn't plan to stay around War Bonnet. Still, some part of her, one of which she had not even been aware of, had apparently hoped that he would change his mind. Maybe it was seeing all those folks coming to him for advice these past couple weeks. Or maybe it was just her own foolishness.

The ranch hands drove off, bumping across the rough terrain in their half-loaded trucks. Rex let the vehicles get some distance away before swinging his bay toward a stand of trees at a little distance.

"There's a pond over here where we can water the horses before heading back to the house."

"We're not going to inspect the third barn?"

"No need. I'll check it later just for form's sake, but I trust Woody."

Callie dutifully nudged Diamond to follow in his wake. They reached the stand of cottonwoods in moments. Rex swung down, loosened the saddle girth and tethered Soldier's reins to a log at the water's edge, leaving the horse to drink before coming to free Bodie from her bonds. The baby immediately reached for the brim of his hat, babbling. Dodging her grasp, Rex returned the favor, releasing the chinstrap on her helmet. Bodie used both hands to shove the thing off her head. It hit the ground with a thud.

Rex laughed and again dodged her attempt to seize his hat. "No trades, sugar."

Thinking that he was asking for a kiss, Bodie planted one on his chin. Laughing, Callie slid to the ground.

"Sugar means kisses to her."

"Right." He wiped his chin. "I should've figured that out by now. She's hot. Let's get this vest off her."

He held her out at an angle, her feet planted against his belly. Callie unbuckled and removed the vest. Bodie clapped her hands.

"Let's have a drink," Callie said, digging into Diamond's saddlebag.

She found a bottle of water and took Bodie, carrying her over to sit on an exposed tree root jutting out of the bank of the pond while Rex saw to the horse. Bodie greedily sucked down the entire eight ounces of water. Then she lay back on her mom's lap and idly kicked a foot, rubbing her eyes with her fists.

"Someone wants a n-a-p."

"I shouldn't have dragged you both out here,"

Rex apologized, carrying over two plastic bottles of sports drink. He'd removed his sunglasses, dropped them into the crown of his hat and left them both sitting in the fork of a leafy branch.

"No, it's okay," Callie told him, taking a bottle after he twisted off the cap for her. She drank long and deep, though she really didn't care for the stuff. He drank as well, one booted foot propped on the tree root next to her. "Woody is right. Your dad's going to be pleased," she told him after a few minutes.

Rex smiled. "Still lots to do."

"He's very proud of you already."

Squinting into the distance, Rex said, "I know. Not sure why, though."

"What do you mean?"

He shrugged and looked intently at his drink. "I sort of rejected the life he meant for me. Then I married poorly. Wound up divorced. And I haven't exactly been faithful with my church attendance. I let my career take precedent, and I've paid the price for that."

"Maybe so, but at least you know it, and you're here now when he needs you most."

"I just have to hope that's enough," Rex said, tilting back his head and finishing off his drink.

In other words, he wouldn't be staying on

the ranch and had every intention of going back to the career that had derailed him in the past. Callie trusted that he would be wiser now. But he would still be far from War Bonnet. He'd probably go back to Tulsa or maybe Oklahoma City.

"We should get back," he said, nodding at Bodie, who drowsed in her mother's lap.

"I'm going to use the shawl to make a sling and carry her against my chest," Callie decided. "She'll be safe enough that way, and she can sleep on the ride back."

"Let me take her," Rex offered. "The brim of my hat will give her some shade."

Callie looked down at her sleepy baby. "All right."

He tightened the cinches on the saddles again while Callie fashioned a sling for her daughter. Bodie whimpered a mild protest as they slung her sideways against Rex's chest, her head nestled in the hollow of his shoulder, but then she reached up a little hand and laid it against his throat, as if feeling the beat of his pulse was all she needed to lull her to sleep.

Callie heard herself whisper, "She loves you."

"I love her, too," Rex said softly. He looked up then, his blue eyes as pale and warm as the summer sky. "I'll miss the two of you if you leave the ranch."

If, not *when.* Confused, Callie dared not reply to that. Anything she said would lay bare her heart, and that simply was not wise. Neither was standing there as he shifted closer, lifted a hand to cup Callie's face and kissed her while her child lay slung across his body between them. Callie kissed him back, falling into the sweetness of it, her hands finding his strong shoulders. She wanted to smile but came closer to weeping. After several long, lovely moments, he broke away and pressed his forehead to hers, breathing deeply.

"I shouldn't have done that," he whispered raggedly. "But Meredith will be here soon."

Callie nodded. Meredith would come, and she would go. She already dreaded the day, but putting it off would only make it harder for everyone when he went away again, for when that happened, she and Bodie would not be going with him. Even if he should ask—and he wouldn't—they would not go. Callie knew herself well enough to know that she couldn't live the way he wanted to live.

She was a small-town girl with a small-town heart, and she wanted nothing else for herself or her daughter. Bodie might choose otherwise when she was grown, and that would be fine, but Callie wouldn't wish it on her. Like Wes, she would understand and endure the choices of her child, but she wouldn't participate.

Sadly, she fetched his hat and sunglasses. He put them on and carefully mounted the horse. Bodie struggled a little, then settled in to snooze. Rex smiled down at her.

"There's a cowgirl if ever I saw one."

Chuckling, Callie climbed onto Diamond, the extraneous gear and empty bottles safely stowed. She took out her phone and snapped some photos, thinking it was too bad that Bodie wouldn't remember this. Then she pushed her sunglasses into place and turned the bay for home.

They ambled into the horse barn about half an hour later, chatting about the possibility of purchasing a four-wheeler to go where the trucks could not, and the horses were too slow to take a busy man. Rex passed Bodie to Callie. Bodie woke enough to protest noisily, then settled with her head on her mother's shoulder. Leaving Rex to deal with the horses, Callie carried her daughter and her wet diaper toward the house, only to draw up short when she saw her father's vehicle parked in the drive.

"Oh, no." She turned back to the horse barn, calling, "Rex, come quick. My dad's here."

He dropped the saddle he was carrying and jogged toward her. "How long's he been here?"

"I have no idea. Go to Wes."

"Woody and Cam are still in the red barn. Ask them to take care of the horses, will you?"

She nodded. "Go."

He went off at a run. She carried Bodie to the workbench in the red barn and called for Woody, who hurried to her.

"Was my father here when you got back?" she asked, quickly beginning to change Bodie's diaper.

"Nope. He drove in about ten minutes ago. I tol' him Rex wasn't around, but he and that idiot Dolent insisted on goin' inside."

"All right. Will you and Cam see to our horses? Rex has gone to run interference, and I need to get in there."

"No problem."

"Thank you."

He doffed his battered, sweat-stained hat. She picked up Bodie and prepared to leave, but he stopped her.

"Miz Callie."

"Yes?"

"Rex has done good here, real good."

"I know."

"Make him stay."

Floored by that comment, Callie felt her jaw

drop. She hugged Bodie to her. "How would you suggest I do that?"

Woody gave her a droll look. "You're a smart cookie. You'll figger it out."

"It's not my place to figure out anything around here," Callie declared.

"Huh," Woody retorted, a world of skepticism in that one syllable. "Seems to me you've made a good place for yourself here, too."

Shaking her head, Callie muttered that she didn't have time for this and hurried to the house. *Make him stay.* As if. Even if she'd had any influence, her father had surely destroyed it in the time it took her to get inside. She heard the shouting before she even reached the porch. Bodie reacted by wailing.

"Now look what you've done," Rex declared, as if he hadn't been shouting, too.

"Me?" Stuart bawled. "You're the one sticking his nose in where it doesn't belong!"

"Those people came to me," Rex said as Callie carried Bodie into the kitchen. "I didn't go looking for them, and if you were more ethical in your personal business practices, you wouldn't be sued."

Callie caught her breath and gaped at Rex. "You're suing my dad?"

"No." He parked his hands at his hips. "I'm

not suing anyone. I'm not even representing anyone who is suing anyone."

"You're not lily-white in this!" Stuart accused.

"People have come to me with contracts they've signed with your father," Rex explained to Callie. "I advised some of them that they had reason to seek redress. They went to other lawyers, and some of them have sued. Knowing that he's in the wrong, Stuart has settled most of the cases out of court."

"Some of them won't settle!" Dolent exclaimed.

"Then maybe the offer is too low," Rex countered.

"You're trying to break me," Stuart growled.

"I'm doing no such thing," Rex retorted, while Wes, Callie noted, sat calmly at the table drinking a cup of coffee. "You're just not used to being beat at your own game," Rex went on. "You've taken advantage of folks around here for so long you think it's your right to do so. Well, it's not. There are laws."

Stuart shook a meaty finger at Rex. "You're not getting away with this, Billings. You hear me? I don't push."

"No one's pushing you," Rex said reasonably. "People are just tired of being taken advantage of."

"So now they're paying you to tell them I'm scamming them," Stuart sneered.

"No one's paid me a dime," Rex pointed out. "Your problem is not with me, Crowsen. Your problem is that you've had your way for too long. You began to think that you always would, that the law didn't apply to you personally. But it does."

"Your problem is that you think you've got pull around here," Stuart scoffed, puffing out his chest, "but you don't."

"All I've got is a working knowledge of the legal system," Rex said, "and the trust and friendship of my neighbors."

"I'm thinking," Wes put in quietly, "that may be more than you've got these days, Stu. Maybe you ought to consider that."

"Maybe you ought to consider just how difficult I can make life around here if I've a mind to," Stuart snarled, nodding at Callie. "Just ask my daughter." With that, he stomped from the room, leaving Dolent to scurry along behind him.

Callie sighed, struggling to hold a fractious Bodie. "He can, you know. When Bo first started asking me out, he was associate pastor at the church in town. Dad got him fired. That's why Bo took the ministry in Turner Falls."

Rex and Wes traded looks. Then Rex stepped forward.

"I'm so sorry he did that, Callie, but Bo was right not to let Stu discourage him."

Wes nodded in agreement. "Stu holds no power over us, Callie. If he did, he'd have used it already."

"He'll find a way to come at you," she warned, looking at Rex.

He shrugged. "What can he do? The Straight Arrow doesn't need Stuart Crowsen to survive. We'll be fine. He's just upset, like I said, because someone's finally beat him at his own game."

Callie wished it was that simple. She didn't doubt that Rex was correct about the contracts; her father wouldn't settle if he hadn't been caught dead to rights. Nevertheless, Stuart Crowsen did not take kindly to being thwarted, and he had a long memory. Rex's advice had cost him money and pricked his pride. Stuart would not let this go. Somehow, someway, he'd find a method to strike at the Billings family— and ultimately it would be her fault.

"I have to bathe Bodie," she said, needing to think.

She hurried away, telling herself that she couldn't let harm come to these good people. She just wasn't sure how to stop it now. Rex had already advised those people about their contracts, and it wasn't as if he'd been wrong about his advice. She'd never expected him to get the better of Stuart like this, though, and for a moment she wondered if Rex and her father were too much alike.

Bo had been her father's exact opposite. That's what she had loved about him, that he was so very different from Stuart. He'd been compassionate and giving, and his quiet, calm strength had flowed from that. Caring nothing for money, unconcerned about security, he'd lived in the moment, trusting God to fulfill each need as it arose. He'd been brave enough to risk his life for others but strong enough to walk away from a fight.

Rex seemed intent on battling her father on Stu's own terms. That being the case, perhaps it was best for everyone that Rex didn't intend to stay around War Bonnet once Wes was strong enough to take over the Straight Arrow again. Doing so would only antagonize Stuart.

Callie didn't even want to think about what might happen to the ranch if Wes *didn't* recover his health. The idea of it passing out of the family appalled her, but it was none of her concern, no matter what Woody said. Like Woody, Cam and Duffy, she was nothing more than hired help around here, despite that kiss beneath the cottonwoods today.

In any event, it would be best if Rex left. It was certainly best for her, because the longer he hung around here, the greater the risk she ran with her foolish heart.

Chapter Ten

The skies poured rain on Thursday, just as the forecast had predicted. With the hay all safely stowed beneath metal roofs, Rex hung around the house, playing chess and cards with his father while Callie used the computer in the study to research straw bale gardening. It was too late to get started for that year, and she wouldn't be around for the next growing season, but she had the idea that she might be able to grow a little garden for her and Bodie with a couple bales wherever they wound up.

When Rex came in to see what she was doing, he showed surprising interest in the subject. The next thing she knew, he was sketching a plan for his mom's old garden spot out behind the house. Callie couldn't help wishing that she could be there to see his garden plan come to fruition, but in truth neither one of them would likely be on hand for that. Still, planning the garden passed the afternoon in a fun, imaginative way, and she learned that Rex loved pickled beets, fried okra and mashed turnips but had no use for Brussels sprouts or kale.

On Friday, while Rex checked to see when the custom cutter might be able to get his equipment into the field of oats, Wes asked Callie to help him shave his head. His hair had started coming out in small chunks, thanks mostly to the pills that Wes took daily, according to Dr. Shorter. Callie made sure to keep Bodie in the room so she could see the transformation taking place and not be shocked by Wes's appearance later. Strangely, Wes looked younger without hair, but his eyebrows had receded to pale, thin lines that looked odd over his light blue eyes.

Rex joked about it when he came in.

"You're going to look younger than me before we're done."

Wes chuckled, running his hand over his smooth scalp. "We'll see. Dr. Shorter says there's no telling what color it will be when it comes back in. My eyebrows, what there is of them, are white. If my hair comes in white—"

"You'll look like a white-haired kid," Rex finished for him, but Callie had seen the sheen of tears in his eyes when he'd first caught sight of his newly bald dad.

"No fear of that," Wes retorted, rubbing a jaw going smooth. "Your sisters are going to freak out."

Nodding, Rex snapped a picture with his cell phone and texted it to them, saying, "Best not to blindside them."

Wes nodded, looking tired. Rex's phone rang, and Callie assumed it was one of his sisters, but to her surprise, he frowned before he answered. "Dennis? What's going on? Yeah, I remember the Shallot case. What do you want to know?"

He carried the phone into the other room, saying he would check his computer files. Wes looked at Callie, his slight eyebrows rising.

"Sounds like his former boss and father-in-law."

Callie turned away to hide her interest. A knock at the front door had her hurrying into the living room to let in Dr. Stark Burns, the local veterinarian.

"Rex around?"

"He's on the phone."

"Any chance I can see Wes? I cleaned up before I came over."

"I guess it'll be okay, but no physical contact, if you don't mind."

"I understand."

She led the tall, lanky, dark-haired animal doctor into the kitchen, where he beamed a smile at Wes without getting too close to the table where Wes sat.

"Now, that's a sight I'm not apt to forget anytime soon."

Wes laughed. "I'm starting a new trend. Next thing I know, you'll be shaving your head."

Burns ran a hand through glossy black hair that showed no glint of silver, though he had to be at least forty. "Yeah. No. I suspect we'd find out I have a pointed head."

Wes laughed again and changed the subject. "How's the herd?"

"Preliminary exam looks good. Going to take a few days to do a detailed inspection. Just thought I'd let Rex know I'd gotten started and see if he wants to ride along on Monday."

"He could be a while," Wes warned, glancing into the dining room.

"Well, just tell him to give me a call," Burns said, hanging his thumbs in his belt loops. "I won't keep you. It was good to see you, Wes."

"You, too, Stark."

"Take care now."

"I'll walk you out," Callie said, and the veterinarian nodded, signaling with his hand for her to go through the doorway first. He fell in beside her in the living room. Then, to her surprise, when they reached the front door, he reached around and held it open for her, giving her a direct look.

Ducking her head, Callie stepped out onto the porch and listened to the sound of the door being pulled closed behind him. He walked to the edge of the porch and turned to face her, leaning a shoulder against the post.

"Wes doing okay?"

"It's hard to say at this point."

Burns nodded. "Horrible disease, cancer."

"Yes."

"Rex has sure done a fine job with this place, though."

"That's what I'm hearing."

"Actually," Burns said, rubbing the bridge of his nose with one long forefinger, "the ranch seems to be running like a top." He linked his fingers and let his hands drop. "Frankly, Wes hasn't been on his game since Gloria died. It's been three years since I surveyed this herd, and when Rex found out, he scheduled a full inspection. He's a natural at this business."

"Good to know," Callie said carefully, though why Burns was telling her this she couldn't imagine.

"Any chance he'll be staying to take over?"

Callie shrugged. "You'll have to ask him that. I'm just hired help around here."

Burns grinned. He was a handsome man in a lean, rugged fashion. "That's not what I'm hearing."

Appalled, Callie blinked. "I don't care what you've heard. That's the fact of it."

The doc folded his arms, staring at her from beneath the crag of his brow. His eyes, she realized, were a deep, dark blue.

"You sit together in church."

"So? He drives me because I don't have a car. It's a condition of my employment."

"Uh-huh. I'm told your little girl calls him 'Daddy.'"

"That's not true!" But she would, given the least encouragement.

"So you're not interested in him at all?" Burns asked skeptically.

"I cook and clean around here," Callie said, aware that her voice shook. "I take care of Wes. That's all."

Stark Burns turned and stepped off the porch, his booted feet thudding on the walkway. "Didn't answer the question," he commented dryly, strolling through the trees.

Callie clamped her jaw, fighting tears. She'd given the only answer that she could. Whirling, she stomped across the porch and swept through the door. She met Rex moving through the living room.

"Did Stark leave?"

"Yes."

"I'm sorry I missed him." He frowned, his gaze narrowing. "You okay?"

"Fine."

"Dad says Stark wants me to call him. Did he say anything else?"

"Yeah," she snapped. "He said you're a natural at ranching and have the Straight Arrow running like a top."

Rex straightened, his eyes widening. "And that has you upset?"

She grimaced. "No, of course not."

Rex smiled. "You know, as a boy, I thought it was all physical labor, but there's more mental aspect in the job than I realized."

"I'm sure," Callie muttered, brushing by him.

"Hang on," Rex said, catching her by the arm. "What did Dr. Burns say to upset you?"

Callie made herself calm down. Putting on a smile, she shook her head. "Nothing. He just wanted to know if you're interested in riding along when he inspects the herd on Monday."

"I'll call him later," Rex said. "Right now I need to do some research on an old case that's reopened. It's what we lawyers call 'found money.'"

Callie tilted her head, asking, "How's that?"

Smiling, Rex spread his hands. "It bills at four hundred dollars an hour."

The figure boggled her mind. "Then please don't let me keep you." Callie turned and walked into the dining room.

Four hundred dollars an hour. To her that sounded like confirmation that Rex would never consider staying around to run the Straight Arrow.

Stark Burns had always struck Rex as a likeable fellow, educated, knowledgeable, hardworking. And single. Suddenly Rex wondered if he ought to be worried about that single part. He'd never thought much about it before, but Stark had kept Callie out on the porch for several minutes on Friday afternoon, and she hadn't quite been the same since. When Rex entered a room, she left it. If he sat down next to her, she got up, and on Sunday morning she actually argued for staying home from church.

"I just think Wes ought not to be alone," she mumbled, her gaze fixed on the breakfast dishes that she carried to the sink.

"He was fine on Wednesday when we went riding."

"If you're worried about your father showing up again," Wes said, "there's an easy fix for that. I just won't answer the door. You can even put up the sign, if it makes you feel better."

Dr. Shorter had provided them with a quarantine sign saying that a cancer patient with a compromised immune system in the house could receive only prescreened visitors. Wes had refused to have it fastened to the door, claiming that it wasn't necessary, and at this point it probably wasn't, though it would be after his next treatment. Rex understood that Wes didn't want to deal with Stuart Crowsen. He couldn't help wondering if Wes had noticed any particularity in the way Stark Burns had dealt with Callie on Friday, but he couldn't think of a way to ask without betraying his own interest in her.

Frustrated, Rex got up from the table, saying, "I'll put up the sign."

Callie sighed, but she didn't argue. He tacked the sign to the front door and went upstairs to get dressed. When he came back down again, freshly shaved and wearing dark jeans with a brown suit jacket and a white shirt, his best boots and a brown felt hat—funny how he'd started to feel underdressed without the cowboy hat lately—Callie and Bodie waited.

Wearing white leggings and a white eyelet blouse beneath a short denim jumper, Callie looked neat and wholesome. Beautiful. Especially with Bodie, decked out in a bright yellow sunflower dress, lolling in the crook of her arm. As soon as she saw him, Bodie launched herself at him, flinging her whole little body in his direction with such determination that Callie almost dropped her.

"Whoa!" Rex caught her in both hands. "Sunshine, you're going to smash that pretty face if you're not careful." He gathered her to him and smiled. "What's that in your hair?" He'd noticed that her fair hair seemed to be thickening lately. As if she understood every word, Bodie reached up and pulled the silk sunflower from her hair. Rex laughed, but Callie scolded her.

"Bodie!" She snatched the flower clip from her daughter's hand and began combing the baby's hair with her fingers. Sliding the clip into place once more, she fixed it and admonished Bodie not to pull it out again. "Leave the pretty alone."

Bodie gave her mom a cheeky grin, pointedly displaying her teeth.

"Has she got new teeth coming in?" Rex asked, shocked to see the glimmer of white on her gums.

"She does."

"Well, look at you, little Miss Overachiever," Rex teased, jostling the baby higher in his arms. Bodie giggled, hunched her shoulders and made a grab for his hat brim. "Uh-uh." Laughing, he dropped her to hip level. Bodie promptly clamped her teeth down on the lapel of his suit jacket.

"Bodie," Callie scolded, prying her off Rex and taking her back.

"Adorable," Rex told Bodie, chucking her under the chin and very nearly getting his finger bitten. She literally snapped her jaws shut just short of his skin.

Finally, Callie laughed. "Be careful for the next few days." She dug in her bag and found a bright orange teething ring, which Bodie went after with great enthusiasm.

Bodie fussed all the way to church. Her front was wet with slobber by the time they pulled up in the dusty parking lot of Countryside Church, despite the soft bib that Callie had fastened around her neck.

The pinkish brick walls of the church, white eaves and cross-shaped front windows needed softening, and not for the first time Rex thought that the place could use some landscaping. Maybe he'd see to it. Some potted evergreens and brightly colored flowers would go a long way toward beautifying the place.

Before he could ask Callie what she thought of the idea, she practically snatched Bodie out of his arms and hurried into the church. Figuring that she wanted to change the little one after dropping her off in the nursery, he shrugged, pocketed the keys and followed, smiling and nodding at others making their way inside.

He removed his hat under the overhang and held open the door for an elderly couple, the Taylors. Mr. Taylor asked about his father, and then, "Where are your girls?"

Rex couldn't help smiling. His girls. He liked that. "Callie and Bodie are already inside."

Others greeted him as he made his way through the small foyer and into the white-on-white sanctuary with its painted woods, brass accents and clear, sun-filled windows. Rex slipped into the usual pew, leaving room for Callie. She liked to sit on the end in case she was called to the nursery. With one paid worker and sometimes a dozen or so children, the church depended on volunteers to help out, and parents with children who used the nursery were always on the list.

The prelude music started, but Callie didn't appear as expected. Rex looked around, thinking that she'd gotten hung up in the nursery. Then he spotted her sitting several rows back and to the side. He motioned to her, but she looked away. Puzzled, he took his hat in hand, got up and went to her. She looked around uncomfortably as he eased past her and dropped down onto the pew beside her.

"You shouldn't," she said softly.

"What?"

"You should go back," she whispered.

"Why?"

"There's talk," she said out of the side of her mouth.

"Talk? About us?"

She nodded and looked away.

Where are your girls? He looked around. No one really seemed to be paying them any mind, though the pastor and a couple deacons had their heads together.

"So? It's nothing bad, is it?"

Callie rocked gently in her seat, not looking at him, her lips compressed. Finally, she shrugged. Rex debated. He could get up and move, or he could stay and stake a claim, more or less. He thought of Stark Burns and A. G. Carruthers and Ben Dolent and other men who seemed to have their eyes on her. Maybe he wasn't sticking around War Bonnet. And maybe, just maybe, he was.

He decided that he wasn't going anywhere, not today, anyway.

Crossing his legs, he shoved his hat onto his

knee and leaned back, his arms stretched out along the edge of the pew. Callie turned wide, questioning eyes on him. Just to be sure she got the message, he wrapped his hand around her shoulder and pulled her closer. She let out a gust of breath, but he saw the smile lurking about her lips and moved his hand to the curve of her neck. Bowing her head, she stiffened, but then she suddenly relaxed against him.

It was a good thing they were in church. Otherwise, he'd be kissing her.

Rex grinned and realized with a shock that—despite his father's illness, the utter chaos of his career, the failures of his personal life and the challenges of keeping the ranch going—he'd never been happier. He actually enjoyed the ranch work. Yes, the physical labor required sometimes exhausted him to the point that he often couldn't pull off his own boots at night. That was only a part of it, however.

Running an operation the size of Straight Arrow Ranch required organization, planning, knowledge, constant education and hands-on leadership. He'd started this job wondering who he was saving the ranch for. It hadn't seemed likely that he or either of his sisters would ever want any part of it. Keeping the ranch going had been nothing more than incentive for Wes to keep fighting his cancer. Now...

Now Rex came home at the end of the day satisfied with his labors, content to eat a fine meal and collapse on the couch, happy to let Callie fuss over him and simply sit in the same room with her. He loved playing with Bodie and helping dress her in her jammies and carry her up to bed. He treasured the way she reached for him, even when he was filthy from the field and sporting a day's growth of beard.

Now he was starting to dread having to turn over the reins to his dad again. One day, Rex knew he could reclaim them, but he wouldn't hope for that because it would mean diminishing his father. On the other hand, maybe he should set up a practice in town and stay on at the ranch. Looking at Callie, feeling her snug against his side, he began to feel that he was finally on the right path.

"Rex, we need to talk to you."

Callie glanced from the pastor to the head deacon and felt her stomach drop. Oh, why hadn't she made Rex take the talk about them more seriously? The very last thing she wanted to do was start gossip about the Billings household.

"Won't take long," the deacon said, nodding politely at Callie. She tried to take comfort from that.

"Sure, sure," Rex said, his hand warm and heavy in the small of her back. "Hon, you go and get the baby. I'll be along directly."

Hon? Callie didn't know whether to stomp his toe or kiss his cheek. Because she didn't know what his play was here, she did neither, turning blindly into the hallway that led to the church nursery. Along the way, she heard whispers and the name Crowsen. Had her father started the rumors? That didn't seem like him, but she'd never seen him this angry, so she really couldn't say what he'd do. Several people stopped her to inquire about Wes's health and to say they were praying for him. She reported on his condition, smiled and thanked them for their concern, but her heart beat so hard and fast that she could barely hear the sound of her own voice.

This was bad. Whatever was happening, she knew in her heart of hearts that it was bad and somehow she was the cause of it.

Cravenly, she took her time getting Bodie's things together. She changed Bodie's diaper and bib, the teething drool having soaked the first one. When she couldn't dawdle any longer, when only she and Bodie remained in the now-darkened space, she carried her daughter into the foyer of the small church and sat down in one of two mostly ornamental chairs flanking the interior door.

The place felt empty, though she knew the custodian was probably still shutting off lights and locking doors while Rex met with the head deacon and pastor in the latter's office. She sat for fifteen, maybe twenty minutes, letting Bodie empty a water bottle. Uncomfortable with the idea of nursing Bodie there in the church foyer, Callie contemplated going out to the truck, but the heat would be unbearable.

Minutes ticked away. Bodie grew fussier. Callie was wondering if the ladies' room had been locked when she heard a door open and the sound of footsteps in the hallway to her left. Bodie sat on the floor between her mother's feet, and she recognized the sound of Rex's voice the instant she heard it.

"I'll speak to Dad as soon as I get home," he said.

"We hate to trouble him," the pastor replied.

"Should've taken his advice to begin with," opined the deacon.

Had Bodie been able to walk, she'd have been halfway across the floor by the time the men reached the foyer. As it was, she moved as fast as she could manage on her hands and knees, fast enough that it took Callie three steps to catch her, bending at the waist, arms outstretched. All three men laughed at the sight. Rex caught the baby in his hands just as Callie swung her up off the floor. Bodie squealed in delight, catching him by the shirtfront and basically climbing him until she could get her hands around his neck.

"She don't like you much," the deacon teased.

"This is my baby girl," Rex said, blowing raspberries against her cheek. Bodie laughed then abruptly switched to squalls.

"She's a hungry baby girl," Callie said, taking Bodie from him and wondering if he'd even heard what he'd said. *My baby girl.*

He picked up his hat from a side table and slid his arm around Callie's waist, saying, "Let's go home."

"Sorry to keep you so long," the pastor told them apologetically as they moved toward the door.

"No problem," Rex assured him. "We'll talk soon."

"Tell Wes we're praying for him."

"Absolutely."

They stepped out into the heat. Rex fit his hat onto his head as they walked toward the truck, his face grim.

"What's wrong?" Callie asked.

"Nothing for you to worry about."

"Tell me."

"In a minute."

They wrestled Bodie into her car seat—she wasn't happy about it—and placated her with a hard teething cookie. She would be a mess by the time they got home, but the poor baby was hungry and hurting. After they climbed into the front seat and Rex got the truck moving, Callie doggedly returned to the subject of the meeting.

"So talk, and don't think to spare me. I heard my father's name mentioned in the hallway."

Rex sighed. "Against advice, the church entered into an unusual loan agreement with your father some time ago, and now Stuart is calling the note due."

"Why?"

Rex took his eyes off the road long enough to face her squarely. "Why do you think?"

Callie closed her eyes. "I'm sorry."

"This is not your fault. He's upset with me."

She shook her head, accepting the inevitable. "Bodie and I will go back into town tomorrow." She'd known this day would come, after all; she just hadn't expected it so soon.

"No," Rex stated flatly, "you won't."

"I've already earned enough to get us out of War Bonnet," she argued, trying not to feel hopeful. "I'll just bide my time until Dad calms down, then we'll slip away."

"No," Rex said again. "We need you at the Straight Arrow." He reached for her hand then, folding his own around it. "I need you. How will we manage without you?"

"M-Meredith——" she began.

"Is not here," he put in, "and even when she is, she's going to have her hands full with Dad. Do you think his next chemo treatment is going to be easier for him?"

Callie shook her head. "Harder," she whispered.

"Meri and I have already discussed it," Rex said. "We're going to need your help even after she arrives."

"I—I don't know, Rex."

"Besides, your leaving now wouldn't change anything," he insisted. "Stu will just keep the pressure on until you do what he wants. You must know your father well enough to know that. The only thing to do now is to stand up to him."

She suspected that Rex was right about this. Once her dad found something that worked, he wasn't going to give it up.

"Still, I can't be the cause for suffering by your family and now even the church, too."

He squeezed her hand. "Like I said, I'm more to blame for this than you are. And I've got some ideas how to deal with it."

"Really?"

Rex nodded. "I'll talk it over with Dad, and see what he thinks, but I feel certain we can foil Stuart's plans."

"I hope you're right."

Lifting her hand, he kissed her fingers. "Trust me. Okay?"

She took a deep breath and nodded, but she had a very bad feeling that she had brought great harm to the Billings family and ranch, not to mention the church. Moreover, she feared that the price for it might be more than her heart could afford to pay. All she could do now, though, was pray—and go as soon as Meredith arrived.

Chapter Eleven

It had been a long time since Rex had sat with his father and prayed with him over a matter. Somewhere along the way he'd stupidly decided that he was too old for a father's counsel, or maybe it had been nothing more than his pride. Rex didn't know anymore; he only knew that he felt a great peace after talking and praying with his dad.

"It's a lot of money, son," Wes said, "but if you're sure you want to do this, I think God will bless the effort."

"Not about that," Rex replied confidently. "I've received material blessings in abundance, but I'm not sure I've been such a good steward of them. I just think it's time I step up."

"I understand," Wes said, clapping Rex on the shoulder. "Maybe this was what God intended when the vote went against me back then. It all seemed so foolish to me. Yet, everyone else thought it a fine idea. It's like your mother said. God always has a plan."

Nodding, Rex smiled and got up to leave his father's room, but first he bent and hugged the old man. "Thanks, Dad."

"For what?" Wes demanded gruffly. "Getting sick? Upending your life?"

"For bringing me home," Rex said, straightening.

Wes turned his head, looking out the window, but Rex had caught the sheen of tears in his faded blue eyes. "God always has a plan," Wes repeated in a gravelly voice.

Rex dropped a hand on his dad's too-thin shoulder. "I just don't want it to involve you dying too soon."

"Might not be soon enough," Wes rumbled.

"Don't say that," Rex scolded.

Wes grimaced. "Don't you think I know that my illness is eating up Straight Arrow reserves? Ever since your mom died I've been wondering why I was holding on here, and now I see you doing so much with this place, and it's more than I ever dared hope for, son. I can't believe the good Lord means to let the ravages of this old body eat up what's been built for you here."

"First of all," Rex lectured, "you're not old.

Second, the ranch means far less to me without you than with you. And third, I've still got plenty of money to invest, Dad, and some ideas about how I want to use it. But I'm not the only Billings with a stake here, you know. I mean to talk to Meri and Ann about a new plan for the Straight Arrow. We'll discuss it in detail when you're feeling better."

He watched his father's eyes fill with tears. Then Wes groused, "In that case, you better let me catch a nap now, before Callie starts pestering me to eat."

Smiling, Rex dropped a kiss on Wes's bald head and went out. Even a proud man deserved to cry in private on occasion.

Rex found more tears in the kitchen. Callie tried to pretend that it was the steam coming out of the oven when she checked her roast, but he knew better.

"I'm sorry. Everything's running late," she said, wiping her face with her apron.

"Not your fault," he told her.

She ignored that, saying, "Dinner should've been done by now. I put the vegetables in as soon as we got home. Hot as it is, I don't know why they're t-taking so lo-ong." Her voice cracked on the last word.

Rex just gathered her into his arms and

turned her into his chest. "Don't cry, sweetheart. Everything's fine."

"It's not," she squeaked. "I don't know the details, but my father's called the note on the church because of *me*. How could he do that?"

Realizing that only a full explanation would suffice, Rex steered her to the table and bodily placed her in a chair. Then he sat down at the end of the table and took her hands in his.

"Some years ago," he began, "the foundation on the church parsonage cracked. The church had bought the property from a third party who didn't hold the mineral rights."

"Typical for Oklahoma," she muttered, wiping her face again.

"Yes. Anyway, they didn't realize that the title restrictions, church ownership coupled with split rights, could make a second mortgage next to impossible. They didn't have the money to repair the damage to the house, which was only going to get worse, so they were in a very difficult situation. They still owed money on the place and couldn't sell it because of its condition, but they couldn't get a conventional sort of loan, so against advice, they elected to borrow from your father."

"Whose advice?" she asked, her brow beetling.

"My father's."

Callie closed her eyes and flipped a hand. "So of course this becomes the perfect vehicle for retribution after I come to work here at the Straight Arrow."

"And after I exposed some of his less-than-legitimate private dealings."

"What happened? Did the church miss a payment or make it late?"

"Several actually. And your dad forgave every one."

"Until now."

Rex nodded slowly. "He went to the pastor on Friday and told him that he had no choice but to call the loan because the church was allowing us, the Billings family, to keep you here under 'illicit and immoral conditions.'" Callie gasped, but Rex went on, "Stuart demanded that the board of deacons pressure us to return you to your 'rightful place' in his household. Otherwise, he'll call the note."

She shot up out of her chair, a look of sheer horror on her face. "How could he…what they must…"

"They told him to go fly a kite," Rex stated calmly, leaning back in his chair and crossing his legs at the ankles. "No one believed it for a minute, Callie. They know you. They know us. They know nothing illicit or immoral is going on here."

She clamped a hand over her mouth, tears streaming from her eyes, and nodded her head. He smiled, relieved that she seemed to believe him.

"Still," she said, wiping her face again, "I can't let him call that note."

"He won't."

"You don't know Stuart Crowsen if you think that," she scoffed. Glancing around, she seemed to be thinking. "I—I'll put up some meals to hold y'all over until Meredith arrives. You…you can get Mrs. Lightner to come in and sit with Wes during the day. It shouldn't take too long. By morning, midday tomorrow, you can d-drive us into town, and this will all be over."

"Until you try to leave town," Rex pointed out gently. "He'll just threaten to call the note again. You know he will."

She shook her head. "Doesn't matter."

"Matters to me," he said softly. "Besides, I thought you understood that you're staying here."

"But—"

Rex got up from the table. "I won't have it, Callie. The only way you leave here is if you *want* to go. Do you want to go?"

She stared at him, her big green eyes filled with worry. "No, but—"

"That's all there is to say on the subject then."

"The church——"

"Has nothing to worry about," he promised, leaning down to flatten his hands on the tabletop.

"How can you say that when you've just told me that they can't pay the loan?"

"They can't," he said, straightening and folding his arms. "*I* can."

She cocked her head as if she hadn't quite caught what he'd said. "You're going to pay off the loan?"

"Yes."

He didn't think her eyes could get any wider, but they somehow did. "How are you going to manage that?"

"By writing a check."

She gaped at him, her jaw dropping, her mouth falling open to show her even white teeth.

"You'd do that to keep us on at the Straight Arrow?"

"Oh, sweetheart," he said, dropping his hands to his hips, "I'd do more than that to keep you and Bodie here."

She needed to sit down before she fell down. Callie felt behind her for a chair, already sinking into it, but there was no chair to be found.

In a flash, Rex shot across the room to fold his arms around her and hold her up.

"You okay?"

Grasping the collar of his shirt with both hands, she shook him. "How much?" she demanded.

"Honey…"

"How much?"

"Almost forty thousand." He said it with a little smile and what almost looked like pride.

"Forty thousand dollars," she breathed.

"I can afford it," he told her, walking her to the table and putting her into the chair again. "I'm happy to do it. Besides," he went on, crouching beside her, "I owe that church."

"Owe the church?"

"When Mom died," he told her, taking her hand in both of his, "our family was in pieces. They took care of us, of everything really. And after, when I couldn't be here, they took care of Dad. Every cold, every virus, every crisis on the ranch, they were here for him. And before you came, they were all that kept us going here, carrying in food, trying to manage the laundry and housework. Of course, it's not just us. The church is God's hands and feet in the community, and Countryside fills that role especially well."

"I've always heard that," Callie conceded.

"So first I do it for God," Rex said, "and then I do it for the church that has been so good to me and my family. I do it for Dad because he needs you here. But I do this for you, too, to keep you out from under your father's thumb. And away from Ben Dolent." She had to smile at that. "And I do it for me," Rex went on, "because my life would be so much less without you and Bodie in it."

"That's temporary at best, though," she pointed out.

"Maybe not. I suspect you can always have a place here at the Straight Arrow if you want it."

Callie smiled, feeling glad and sad at the same time. "That's lovely, but you're going—"

"Nowhere," he said, pushing up to his full height again. "I'm home, and I'm not finding any reason to be anywhere else." Callie knew that she was gaping again, but she couldn't seem to help herself. "I'm not going anywhere," he stated, "and Stuart Crowsen had better get used to the idea." He cupped her chin in his hand then, gently closing her mouth. "You, too."

She stared up at him for several seconds before Bodie's thin wail pierced her awareness.

"Oh. The baby." Callie got to her feet, and the aroma of pot roast with all the fixings hit her. "And dinner."

"I'll get the baby," Rex said. "You take care of dinner."

Flustered, Callie started toward the oven, only to turn back. "Uh, she's going to need changing. I'd better go."

"I think I can change a diaper," Rex said, waving her back toward the oven. "I've watched you do it often enough now."

The timer dinged, and Callie grabbed a pair of pot holders, calling, "I'll just take this out of the oven and come up."

"I've got it," Rex assured her, striding toward the stairs.

Callie pulled the heavy roasting pan from the oven and lifted the lid, her mind whirling. The meal seemed ready at last. All that remained was to dish everything up and thicken the gravy while the bread browned. Bodie's crying stopped, so Callie kept working, and by the time she poured the gravy into the serving dish, Rex was back, a freshly diapered Bodie in his arms.

For once Bodie wanted her mama, so Rex handed her off then shifted food to the table before calling his dad. He pulled the bread from the oven while Callie mashed roasted potatoes, carrots and beans with milk for Bodie. She would feed her a little solid food now and nurse her later.

Rex said the blessing over the meal, and Callie heard a peaceful new strength in his voice that both thrilled and frightened her a little. He was nothing like her late husband had been. Bo had prayed easily and eloquently in public, but in retrospect, Bo seemed like an idealistic boy compare to Rex. Yet, the strength with which Rex met her father's machinations both thrilled and, if she was honest, unnerved Callie a little. Oh, Rex had his soft side, too. She saw it every time he played with Bodie or when he helped his dad bathe or dress, but she couldn't ignore his toughness.

In some ways he seemed a combination of Stuart and Bo. She just didn't know if that was a good thing or a bad one.

For one thing, how was she supposed to resist *this* Rex? How did she *not* fall in love with him?

She wanted to believe that he was falling in love with her, too, but what did she have to offer him besides cooking and housekeeping services? And what did she do with the sudden disloyalty that she felt toward sweet, gentle Bo?

Her emotions were so conflicted that, on Monday evening, when Rex dragged in so exhausted that Callie wondered if he could make it to the dinner table, she resorted to scolding him.

"Are you trying to make yourself sick? You left early and skipped lunch today."

"Just trying to get the sorghum in the ground."

"I thought you were about to *harvest* sorghum. Now you're planting it?"

"We're harvesting the early crop. We're planting the late fodder."

"I don't understand. Why not just buy feed like everyone else. It's because of me, isn't it? Because my father won't sell you what you need."

Rex chuckled. "Not even close, darlin'. We've done some research, Dad and I, and grass-fed beef is far healthier than beef fattened on engineered feeds. Straight Arrow is abandoning the feedlot. I've talked to Stark Burns about it, and he's completely on board. No antibiotics, except to treat ill animals. From now on, everything we feed our herd, we raise right here on the ranch, organically. Eventually, we'll have our own brand, Straight Arrow Beef."

Callie literally marveled. "Rex, that's...that's brilliant."

He smiled tiredly. "Well, Dad and my sisters are on board. Guess we'll see. Now, if I don't move, I'm going to drop where I stand."

Nodding, she hurried toward the kitchen. "Dinner is ready when you are."

"I'll be along."

He came in buttoning a clean shirt a few minutes later and managed to eat a full meal, but then he fell asleep on the sofa in the living room while she was cleaning up. She hated to wake him, but he needed to go to bed, so she gently shook his shoulder.

"Chloe," he said, jerking up straight in his seat.

"What?"

He rubbed his eyes with the heels of his hands. "Huh?"

"You said, 'Chloe,' I think."

Shaking his head, he slid to the edge of the couch, mumbling, "Uh, I f'got t' tell you 'bout her."

Sighing, he got up, but he swayed so badly that Callie had to catch him, encircling his waist with her arms.

"You need to go to bed."

"Yeah."

"Let me help you."

"Always," he muttered, dropping an arm about her shoulders and sounding half drunk. "Don' know what I'd do withou' you."

She moved him toward the foyer and the stairs.

"Up we go."

"I hope."

He reached out and grasped the rail, pulling as she literally pushed, and together they slowly climbed the stairs. Two steps from the top, Bodie began to whimper; by the time Callie got Rex to his bedroom door, Bodie was wailing.

His head turned, and he swayed in that direction, but Callie pushed him through his bedroom door even as he asked, "What does the baby want?"

"Me."

"Smart girl." He sighed, as she guided him to the narrow bed. Callie pushed, and he plopped onto the side of the bed. "Kiss her f' me," he mumbled as Callie picked up his foot and pulled off his boot.

"I will." She dropped the first boot and went after the other.

"Here," he said, catching her face in his hands and guiding it to his. He kissed her sweetly. "Mmm. Thank you."

"Go to sleep," she whispered as he collapsed onto the bed.

Sighing, he closed his eyes and drifted away even as her daughter shrieked from the other room. He was too big for that bed. Callie glanced around. He didn't belong in that bed or in this room. This room was meant for a boy, not a grown man who worked until he collapsed. It seemed to her that everything had gone all topsy-turvy at the Straight Arrow, that nothing was quite as it should be. How much of it was because of her? Brushing tears from her eyes, she went out and closed the door, hurrying to take care of her demanding little daughter.

He was up and gone again before daylight, no breakfast other than the toast and coffee that he fixed for himself, though she rose early to try to catch him. Callie made up her mind that she would grab the car keys from his dresser and drive his expensive two-seater out to the field if he didn't come in for lunch. He'd probably have a fit. She hadn't even seen the car. It sat under a temporary cloth cover beneath the big tree out behind the house, but she knew that it was an expensive, low-slung sports car completely unsuited to ranch life. Still, if he didn't take care of himself, she would do what she had to.

She didn't have to make that drive, but not for the reason she'd hoped.

As she was in the middle of lunch preparations, she heard the sound of tires on the dirt road outside the house. Assuming that Rex had come in for the midday meal, she relaxed, but then she heard unusual footsteps on the porch and a knock at the door. Glancing at Bodie to be sure she was fine in the playpen, Callie cleaned her hands and moved cautiously into the foyer to answer the knock.

A stunning redhead, her long hair draped over one shoulder, smiled and fluttered a slender, perfectly manicured hand in greeting. She was tall, or seemed so in high heels, and wore an obviously expensive white suit with a pencil-thin skirt and formfitting jacket. Gold dripped from her wrist, fingers, throat and earlobes. Callie felt like a rock next to a polished gem.

"Hello," said this woman in a silky voice, her perfectly made-up, violet eyes sparkling with curiosity. "I'm Chloe Gladden."

"Chloe Gladden," Callie echoed stupidly. *Chloe. I forgot to tell you about her.*

"I believe Rex is expecting me."

"Rex, uh, isn't here."

"No?" The woman shifted, bringing a slender briefcase from her back to her side, its narrow strap slung over one shoulder. "Well, I am a little early. I imagine he'll arrive soon. Should I wait out here?"

Callie swallowed down the response she wanted to make and backed up, opening the door wide. "No, no. Please come in."

"Thank you."

Chloe Gladden strolled gracefully inside. On closer inspection, she seemed a bit older than Callie had assumed, but she was slender, fit and very attractive.

"Please take a seat. I'm sorry that I must ask you to remain in this room. Rex's father is seriously ill and shouldn't be exposed to anyone outside the immediate family."

"Yes, I know," Chloe Gladden said warmly, sinking down onto the edge of the sofa. "How is Wes?"

Callie found it surprisingly difficult to speak for some reason. "Um, as well as can be expected."

"Oh, I'm glad, for Rex's sake as much as Wes's."

Trying to smile, Callie asked, "How…how do you know Rex and Wes?" She knew the question was out of line, but she couldn't help herself.

Chloe Gladden sat up a little straighter, if such a thing was possible. "Didn't Rex tell you? I'm his mother-in-law."

Mother-in-law? "I thought Rex was divorced," Callie blurted out.

Chloe Gladden smiled smoothly. "Yes. Of course. Technically I'm his *ex*-mother-in-law."

If this was the ex-mother-in-law, Callie thought bitterly, she never wanted to lay eyes on the ex-*wife*.

"If you'll excuse me," she said quietly, "I need to get back to work."

Chloe Gladden smiled benignly, the type of smile that bespoke an easy comfort with servants. "Of course."

Turning blindly, Callie hurried from the room, bruising her heart with every step.

Chapter Twelve

"You've looked better," Chloe said bluntly, following Rex into the study.

Hanging his hat on the wall peg, he chuckled, well aware that he was dirty, unshaved and uncombed. "No doubt, but I've never been happier, Dad's health notwithstanding."

"I guess that means you're not coming back to the firm."

Surprised, he walked around the desk. "I thought we'd already settled that."

Chloe shrugged. "Your talents have been missed. In all areas."

Knowing perfectly well that she referred to her daughter, Rex snorted. "I find that hard to believe."

In a gesture of studied submissiveness, Chloe sank down onto the edge of the chair in front of the desk, her hands folded atop the slender, expensive briefcase in her lap. "Amy wonders if you would consent to meet with her. She wants to talk, to apologize."

With his hands at his waist, Rex looked Chloe straight in the eyes. "There's nothing to talk about." He pulled open a desk drawer and removed a file, tossing it onto the blotter. "You can tell her that her apology is accepted, and that's the end of it." He pushed the file forward. "The Shallot file."

Chloe reached out and picked it up. "You've moved on."

"I've moved on," he confirmed. "The invoice is attached to the inside of the file jacket."

Flipping open the file, Chloe glanced at the invoice and raised an eyebrow before sliding the file into her briefcase. Relaxing back into her chair, she lifted her gaze.

"Callie, is it?"

Smiling, Rex went to the study door. "Callie!" he called.

Within five seconds she appeared, Bodie on her hip, a dishtowel on her shoulder. "Yes?"

"Sweetheart, would you mind if Chloe and I have lunch in here? We have work to do."

She glanced curiously into the study, while Bodie reached for him. "No problem."

"Thank you." He kissed Bodie on the forehead, which allowed her to get one hand on his collar and the other in his hair. He laughed. "Hey, monkey, I'm too dirty for you."

"Let go," Callie admonished gently, trying to pry her off.

"Oh, let her stay until you bring lunch," he said, changing his mind. He pulled the towel from Callie's shoulder as he gathered Bodie into his arms.

Her forehead furrowing, Callie asked, "Are you sure?"

He nodded, arranging the towel across his chest and holding Bodie against it. "She'll have to have a bath afterward."

"She has to have a bath anyway," Callie said. Leaning close, she whispered, "Lunch is just sandwiches, though. Why didn't you warn me?"

"Great," he said heartily, ignoring the latter. "Bring it on." He hadn't warned her because he'd been too tired to think the previous evening, and he'd completely forgotten to leave her a note this morning. If Chloe hadn't called for directions when she'd reached War Bonnet, he'd still be in the field now. For apology, he kissed Callie on the forehead. He really wanted to kiss her on the lips, but he feared that would embarrass her in front of Chloe.

Frowning, she went off to put together the meal. Rex carried Bodie into the room and sat down behind the desk with her, turning her so that her back rested against his towel-covered chest. She stared at his guest, her fist in her mouth, drool sliding down her arm. What passed for shock widened Chloe's carefully arranged lawyer's expression.

"You'll have to forgive her," Rex said smugly, jiggling Bodie's bare feet. "She's not much of a conversationalist, especially right now. She's teething like crazy. Aren't you, princess?" Bodie tilted her head back, yanked her fist from her maw and gave him a grin that showed all four of her tiny teeth. "She is, however, quite entertaining." As if to prove the point, Bodie suddenly pitched forward and made a grab for the ink pen beside the blotter. Rex calmly flicked it out of her reach.

She flipped over and crawled up his chest. Rex leaned back in his chair, laughing as she bounced up and down on his thighs, her chubby knees digging into his ribs.

"Good grief, you mean it," Chloe said. "You're not coming back."

"No, I'm here to stay," Rex told her, looking around Bodie as she smacked both hands on the top of his head. "Home has never been sweeter." He kissed Bodie's belly, where a strip of skin showed between the hem of her little T-shirt and the top of her diaper. She squealed with delight, tickled by his whiskers, and patted herself while he held her steady with both hands. "Work's never been more enjoyable. Or harder."

Chloe shook her head. "Surely you're not giving up the law."

"Nothing of the kind," Rex said, tucking Bodie into the curve of his arm. "I'm thinking of specializing in ranching and cattle issues. It's what I know best, after all, which is why your firm called me in on the Shallot mess. Though I may open an office in War Bonnet."

"Well, you've certainly got the chops for that specialization," Chloe conceded. "And Callie?"

"Haven't worked that out yet," he admitted. Callie suited him somehow, she and Bodie, but he wasn't sure the feeling was mutual. That, however, wasn't why he'd asked Chloe to come. "I've got some things to clear up first."

"And *that's* why I'm here," Chloe guessed.

Rex smiled. "You did say that you wanted to pick up that file, too."

Glancing around the room, Chloe said, "I wouldn't have to if you'd buy a printer with a scanner."

Laughing, Rex wrestled Bodie down into his lap. "It's on my list of things to do, right below get the sorghum planted and harvest the oats and right before *buy a new truck*."

Chloe gaped at him. "Will wonders never cease?"

"You know what they say. You can take the boy off the ranch, but you can't take the ranch out of the boy. Or something to that effect."

Laughing dryly, Chloe asked, "So what do you need?"

"It involves a church and a loan that I want paid off anonymously."

Chloe stared at him for five full seconds. "She must be something, this Callie."

"Not something," Rex said softly. "More like everything." But he couldn't be her escape from her father any more than he'd been Amy's gift to hers.

If he and Callie couldn't be together because they were right for each other, because they belonged to each other, were made for each other, then they shouldn't be together at all.

He'd tried to tell himself that it didn't matter how they came together, only that they *be* together, but experience had shown him the folly of that. Besides, Callie's late husband had been an exemplary character, heroic, even. A man like that could be difficult to live up to. If Rex was to risk his heart again, he had to know beyond any doubt this time that he was chosen and loved purely for himself. As sweet and caring and affectionate as Callie was, he could see those doubts in her eyes.

That didn't stop him from letting everyone around them think they were a couple. Even the ranch hands had started to assume that they were "courting," as Woody put it. Stark Burns called it "getting serious." Rex had bluntly told the pastor and head deacon that Callie was the finest, most moral and completely adorable woman he'd ever known. He'd made his personal interest plain while defending her reputation, even worrying aloud that he might not be worthy of her. Both knew that she'd been married to a minister who'd died in an act of heroism, though Stuart talked about Bo Deviner as if the man had been a bounder after his money. At least Rex could escape that accusation. He hoped.

Callie came in with two plates of food, flatware, napkins and drinks on a tray. Her sandwiches stood two inches thick and came accompanied by a colorful, fresh fruit salad, bread-and-butter pickles, pretzels, cold iced tea and some dainty white cookies. She off-loaded the tray and set it aside, reaching for Bodie just as Rex sneaked the baby a bite of cookie.

"Don't you dare," Callie scolded softly.

"Aw, come on," Rex protested, popping the remaining cooking in his mouth, where it literally melted. "They're so good."

"You spoil her," Callie said, parking Bodie on her hip.

"You spoil me," Rex countered with a smile.

Callie glanced uneasily at Chloe, who was picking delicately at her fruit. "I don't. And if I do, it's because you work too hard."

"Look who's talking," he retorted with a wink, popping another cookie into his mouth.

Shaking her head, Callie leaned over, snatched the dishtowel off his chest and spun on her heel.

"Close the door, hon," he called as she exited the room. She shot him such a look that he wanted to laugh, or get up and hug her. Instead he ate another cookie then grinned very broadly as she carefully, quietly closed the door.

"Boy, you have got it bad," Chloe drawled.

"Uh-uh," Rex corrected, picking up his sandwich. "I have got it good. Very good." *Please God*, he prayed silently, *let it last*.

They talked out a solution to his loan issue over lunch. Chloe jotted down the particulars on a notepad. Then they went online using Rex's laptop and made the necessary financial transfers.

"I'll take care of it before I leave town," she promised.

Callie tapped on the door, asking if she could come in for the dishes.

"Sure," Rex called, lounging back in his chair. She opened the door and came in. He'd stacked the dishes on the tray and left them on the end of the desk. Smiling, he said, "We're just about through here, babe."

She widened her eyes at him, picking up the tray.

"Speaking of babes…" Chloe said, her voice laced with humor.

Callie smiled tautly. "Bodie is napping upstairs." She looked pointedly at Rex, adding, "And Wes is sleeping in his room."

In other words, he should have looked in on his dad before he'd closeted himself in here with Chloe. Point taken.

"I'll look in on him when we're done."

Callie nodded, the slightest of smiles on her face, and carried the dishes from the room.

"Keeps you in line, doesn't she?" Chloe observed wryly.

"With great ease," Rex admitted, a grin breaking across his face, "and I don't even care if she knows it." Chloe laughed. "Back to business. What do I owe you for your help today?"

Chloe reached into her bag and drew out the file he'd given her earlier. Opening it, she reached inside and pulled out the invoice stapled to it. "Let's just call it even, shall we?" She crumpled the invoice in her hand and tossed it onto the desktop.

"That's very generous, Chloe. Thank you."

"It'll earn me brownie points at the firm when they don't have to pay you for this," she said dismissively, returning the file to her bag.

A few minutes later, he walked her to the door, delicately kissed her cheek, ignoring her wrinkled nose, and sent her on her way before going in search of Callie. He found her in the laundry room, shoveling wet clothes into the dryer. She straightened and turned when he came into the room.

"All done?"

He nodded. "She's going to handle paying off the church loan for me. That's why I asked her to come. That and she needed to pick up the case file I prepared for her firm last week. Um, remind me to buy a new printer with a good scanner function."

"So she's a lawyer, too."

"Yes."

"But why do you need a lawyer?"

"For the same reason that a doctor needs a

doctor. It would be foolish to represent myself, especially when I'm trying to remain anonymous."

Callie blinked at that. "Why do you need to be anonymous to pay off the church loan?"

"I don't need to be," he said. "I *want* to be."

She fluffed her bangs, showing him a beetled brow. "Why?"

He shrugged. "Just seems the right way to handle it. What is it Matthew says? When you give, don't let your left hand know what your right hand is doing. Give in secret."

"'Then Your Father, who sees what is done in secret, will reward you,'" Callie quoted.

"I don't want to be rewarded," Rex said. But didn't he? Wasn't he on some level competing with at least the memory of her late husband? He felt a certain shame at the realization of that, but at the same time, common sense told him that Bo Deviner no longer walked in this world while Callie did. She deserved and needed someone to care for her. Why not him?

He stepped closer, realized that he was still covered in dirt and no doubt smelled like a goat, so he simply skimmed his fingertips along her jawline before saying, "I'll probably be late tonight. Don't hold dinner for me."

She looked down. "You can't keep up this pace for much longer."

"I won't have to."

"Go see your dad. I'll pack you a snack."

Leaning close, he whispered into her ear, "Cookies."

Laughing, Callie pushed him away. Ridiculously pleased with himself, Rex went out to slip into his dad's room and watch him sleep for several long seconds. When he returned to the kitchen, Callie handed him a thermos, an apple and a Baggie of cookies.

"Come home as soon as you can."

"I always do." He smiled, adding softly, "I always will."

He could tell that she didn't quite believe that. Why should she? No matter. She would learn how ardently he meant those words, provided he could keep her around long enough.

Strangely, the more Rex talked of planting his roots in War Bonnet, the more Callie feared that her time for leaving quickly approached. Moreover, she knew that Rex would not be paying off the church loan if she hadn't come to work at the Straight Arrow. It seemed to her that she had brought more difficulty than good to the Billings family, and she felt terribly conflicted about her growing attraction to Rex.

Bo had drawn her to him with his quiet, peaceful presence. He'd made her feel safe and treasured. There were elements of that with Rex, too, but he excited her in ways that she found disturbingly addictive. Even as she fought those feelings, she craved them, too, and that made her question her own judgment. Worse, she didn't know where to turn for advice, so she simply prayed on the matter. Then Wes called her to task.

"What's troubling you, girl? And don't tell me it's nothing. I'm sick. I'm not stupid." He sighed as he sank down onto the side of his freshly made bed and kicked off his slippers. "Talk."

Callie shook her head, gathering the discarded bed linens, and gave him a half-truth. "I guess I'm just waiting for the next round in this ongoing war between my dad and Rex."

"Hmm." Wes lifted his feet onto the bed and leaned back. "I wouldn't worry none. Rex can outfox old Stu."

"Rex is as clever and resolute as my father, that's true."

"And you don't think that's a good thing?" Wes asked, clearly hearing what she hadn't said.

Callie bit her lip, hugging the laundry to her. "Do you?"

Wes chuckled. "You know, I admire a lot about your father. I admit he sometimes lets his business sense get the better of him, but he's done plenty good around town, and he's made a lot out of nothing. Why, I remember when your dad first started in business." Shaking his head, Wes grinned. "His little old grocery wasn't much more than a convenience store back then. He built that up, and then he bought out the Feed and Grain and improved that, and when the bank faltered, he stepped in there and put it to rights. Soon, he owned most of the town. He was well on his way to being the big fish in our little pond when your mother died." Sighing, Wes went on in a more somber tone. "After that, he seemed to pour all his grief and fear into making money. I remember him telling me that the best thing he could do for you was to leave you a fortune."

"But life isn't just about material things," Callie argued, realizing as she said it that those words had become a mantra over the years, one her father had heard many times. And ignored.

"Of course, it's not," Wes agreed, "but I think Stuart didn't know what else to do for you, Callie. Believe me, I understand his dilemma. I have daughters myself. I was also blessed to have a wife to help me navigate the confusing stages between infancy and womanhood with my girls. And it's still pretty much a mystery to me. I admit that I'd have been lost without Glory to help me raise my kids, and that includes Rex." Wes rubbed a hand thick and heavy with years of hard toil over his bald head. "Except for those few years, Stu didn't have the luxury of a wife at his side, and he did love your mom."

"He never talks about her," Callie said softly. "What was she like?"

"You," Wes told her succinctly. "Calm, strong, smart, pretty."

Callie smiled, blushing. "I've always wondered how I could miss someone I never really knew, but I do. I always have."

"Why, naturally you would. That's just human nature." Wes stared into the distance, musing, "Jane balanced Stuart somehow. The day of the car wreck, I'd never seen anyone so devastated. I thought of him the day my Glory died and how blessed I was to have her for so many years." He looked at Callie then, saying, "I understood Stu better that day. I don't think he's ever gotten over losing Jane. Seems to me one reason for his controlling ways is that he doesn't want you to go through life living with that kind of pain and loss."

"And yet, here I am doing that very thing," Callie said softly.

Wes nodded. "And he's trying to fix it."

Shocked, Callie sighed. "Poor Dad. He can't fix it. If he could, I'd let him. Doesn't he know that?"

Reaching out to pat her hand, Wes said, "You'll find out for yourself one of these days how very hard it is to let go of your children and give them over to God. But it's like my Glory always said, God gives us the free will to choose our own way, and that's the example we have to follow with our own children."

"I know Dad thinks I was wrong to marry Bo," Callie said thoughtfully, "but I'd do it again, even knowing how it would end."

"I'm glad for you then," Wes told her. "I just hope you can understand your father's motivations a little better now. And I hope you can see how much there is to admire about Stuart Crowsen. And my son. They're strong men who make things happen, Callie. This world needs men like them."

Callie smiled. "Those aren't the only two admirable men around here."

Wes linked his fingers and tucked them behind his head, grinning. "Of course not." He winked, then he closed his eyes.

Laughing, Callie carried the laundry from the room. With a father like that, Rex couldn't be *too* much like Stuart, which just made her situation all the more acute.

Callie knew that she had some thinking and praying to do, where both her father and Rex were concerned.

Was it possible that she had misunderstood her father all these years? Might this new insight help them come to an understanding at long last, and if they could manage that, might she and Bodie be able to stay around War Bonnet long enough for something meaningful to develop between her and Rex?

She still felt a prick of guilt, as if thinking of even the possibility of a future with another man was a betrayal of Bo. Yet, she knew that her late husband would not begrudge her happiness, help or love. She didn't doubt that she could—probably already did—love Rex, but she had no assurance in her heart that he could or would love her.

Oh, she knew that he was attracted to her, but that was not the same thing as true love, and neither was gratitude or pity. What she didn't know was if he truly meant to stay on at Straight Arrow Ranch or if he was God's will for her.

She supposed that time would tell, but her time here could be very limited. Ironically, now that she wanted to grasp time and make it stand still, it seemed to slip through her hands like sand.

If she could make peace with her father, convince him to back off his plans for her future and stop trying to force Ben Dolent on her, she could stay around War Bonnet. If, however, her father insisted on trying to bully everyone around them until she did as he wanted, then she'd have no choice but to take her daughter and move away.

She began to pray that God would give her the means to reach him. Doubt argued that she'd never been able to do so before, but that was before she'd known how like her mother she was.

Like mother like daughter. Calm, strong, smart. She hoped.

Chapter Thirteen

Callie smiled at Rex when he appeared in the doorway of the kitchen.

"You're home very early today."

She'd made a concerted effort lately to be welcoming and helpful without being too blatant about it. He'd been sweet lately, especially with Bodie and his father. It helped that he wasn't working himself to the bone anymore. Now that the sorghum had been planted and a few weeks remained before the rye and barley harvest could begin, Rex had been seeing shorter days, but he'd never before walked in just after two o'clock in the afternoon.

He leaned a shoulder against the casement of the doorway and lifted a brow, saying, "I thought I'd get a shower and clean up before your father arrives."

The bottom dropped out of Callie's stomach. "My father?"

Rex nodded and folded his arms. "He phoned me on my cell phone earlier. Said he was in need of legal services."

She shouldn't have been surprised, but somehow Callie hadn't expected things to play out quite this way.

"You couldn't refuse?"

"Thought about it," Rex admitted. "Then I decided it might be best just to find out what he's got up his sleeve."

Tilting her head, Callie considered a moment, then nodded. "You're right."

Rex grinned. "A man loves a woman who tells him that he's right."

Callie burst out laughing. A part of her hoped that he meant that literally, but she knew very well that he was teasing. Bodie chose that moment to use the rail of the playpen to pull up to her feet and call out to Rex.

"Hiii."

Still smiling, Rex strolled over and crouched down beside the playpen. "Hi, baby. How's my girl this afternoon? Being good for Mama today?"

"Ma-ma," Bodie repeated, reaching through the wood slats for him. He caught her hand and kissed her palm.

"I can't play now, baby. I've got to shower. I love you, though. You're such a cutie. I'll be back." He pushed up to his full height, bent at the waist and kissed her on the top of the head. She screeched furiously when he walked away again, moving toward the back hallway and the stairs. Rex took her display of temper in stride, saying, "I need to hurry. He'll be here by three."

"I'll make coffee," Callie said, trying to placate Bodie with a stuffed toy. Her dad loved his coffee.

"Got any cookies to go with that?"

"No, but I baked banana bread this morning."

"You're perfect," Rex called as he began climbing the stairs.

"As if," she shouted over the baby.

"Don't argue with me, woman," he shouted back.

Smiling and shaking her head, Callie went to the pantry for coffee grounds. Bodie flopped down onto her bottom and started to cry.

"Oh, hush," Callie told her. "He'll be right back." Then she started to pray that whatever her father had up his sleeve would not harm the Billings family or any other innocent party.

By the time Rex came downstairs again, his damp hair curling around his collar, the cuffs of his pale blue shirt rolled back to his elbows, Bodie had calmed. Callie had sliced the dark, moist, nut-rich bread and arranged it on a platter, made a pot of fresh coffee and set out plates, forks and napkins. She'd also taken a cup of coffee and a thick slice of the bread to Wes, whom she'd told of the afternoon's development.

"This ought to be good," he'd chortled. "Leave my door open, why don't you? Next best thing to being the proverbial fly on the wall."

Callie rolled her eyes, but she'd left Wes's bedroom door wide open.

Rex took a slice of the bread and carried it into Wes's room. The two chatted while they waited for Stuart to arrive. They didn't have to wait long. Callie was watching through the window over the kitchen sink when the Cadillac pulled up. With her heart pounding, she went at once to tell Rex.

"They're here. Looks like Ben is with him."

Rex shrugged and said, "I'll let them in." As he passed her, he patted her shoulder and added, "Relax, sweetheart. Everything's going to be fine."

Callie looked at Wes, who gave her a thumbs-up. She went to check once more that all was in readiness.

As soon as the three men walked into the kitchen, Bodie began to clamor for attention. Callie picked the baby up, settling her in her usual place on her hip as Stuart nodded a greeting.

"Dad. You're looking well."

He skimmed his gaze over her and Bodie, saying nothing, while Ben shuffled his feet nervously behind him. Rex extended an arm in invitation.

"Let's all have a seat." He pulled out a chair for Callie, but she shook her head.

"Sit, daughter," Stuart barked. "This concerns you."

Callie lifted her chin, about to tell him that she wanted no part of whatever scheme he was launching now, but then she felt Rex's hand at the small of her back and remembered all that Wes had told her about her father and his motivations.

She bowed her head, nodded and said, "All right. Can I get anyone a cup of coffee first? There's freshly baked banana bread on the table."

"I'll have a cup," Rex replied, though he usually preferred iced tea at this time of day.

"Me, too," Ben joined in, taking a plate and helping himself to the sweet bread.

Stuart scowled and shook his head, then said, "Coffee wouldn't hurt."

Callie smiled to herself, knowing what a coffee addict her father was. When she returned to the table, three cups of coffee balanced on a small tray, her father was picking at a piece of banana bread with his fingers, the fork that he'd used to serve himself abandoned on the edge of the plate.

Rex had taken the chair next to hers. When Callie sat down, Bodie immediately tried to climb into his lap. Callie shifted the baby to her other side, where she spied Ben's high-crowned hat resting, brim up, on the table. The look of horror on Ben's face as he moved the hat out of Bodie's reach made Callie bite her lips to hide her smile.

Stuart didn't waste any more time on pleasantries. He glared at Rex and demanded, "Where's Wes?"

"In bed," Rex replied neutrally, "where he belongs. I'm afraid Dad still has to keep his distance from company because of the chemotherapy."

Clamping his jaw, Stuart took his time choosing his words. "I'm sorry to hear that. Guess we should be thankful he's well enough to go around paying off loans."

Callie tried not to breathe while Rex calmly

sipped his coffee, set aside the mug and folded his arms against the tabletop. "What loan would that be?"

Stuart glared. "You know what loan! The Countryside Church loan. Don't take me for a fool, Rex Billings."

Rex shook his head, pushed back his chair, got up and walked out of the room and down the hall to his father's bedroom door. "Dad," he asked loudly enough for all to hear, "did you pay off a loan for Countryside Church?"

"No, I did not," Wes answered just as loudly.

Rex walked back to the table. He sat down again and pulled his chair up to the table. "Now, if that's what you came to find out," he said to Stuart, "you have your answer."

Stuart frowned, his eyes narrowing. "If it wasn't him, then it was you."

"I'm not even a member of that church," Rex pointed out evenly.

Callie kept her face straight and her mouth shut, until her father turned his glare in her direction. Then she said, "Don't look at me. I haven't paid off any loans."

Flattening his mouth, Stuart picked up his coffee mug and sat back in his chair. "Actually, there's another matter I wanted to talk to you about," he said to Rex, "a personal one." He looked at Ben, who ducked his head, picked up his plate and started to eat with great gusto. "I need a lawyer to draw up adoption papers," Stuart said with a sly smile.

Panic hit Callie in a wave.

Rex glanced at her, echoing, "Adoption papers."

Callie wanted to get up and run away, but she feared that her legs wouldn't hold her. She grabbed Bodie's hand in hers. The baby had been entertaining herself by patting Callie's chin in an attempt to get her to open her mouth.

Gulping down her panic, Callie snapped, "You cannot have my daughter!"

Her father gaped at her before demanding, "How would I take care of a baby? I could barely take care of you after your mother died, and you were practically dressing yourself. Babies take live-in help, and live-in help is not easy to come by around here, as you ought to know."

"Then what are you talking about?" Rex asked sharply. "Bodie is the only child here that we know about."

"It's possible to adopt grown heirs," Stuart said smugly. "I've done my research. It's rare, but it happens."

"Grown heirs," Rex mused, tapping his chin and staring at Stuart. Ben suddenly set aside his empty plate with a clatter and seized his coffee, slurping loudly. Rex switched his gaze, fell back in his chair and shook his head. "Now, there is one for the books."

Confused, Callie spread a look around the table. "What? What's going on?"

"Your dad is going to adopt Ben," Rex drawled.

Callie realized she'd dropped her jaw when Bodie used her free hand to reach into her mouth and tried to pluck out her teeth.

"That's right!" Stuart exclaimed, leaning forward to make his point with Callie. "What I've built matters. To this community, if not to you."

Callie pulled Bodie's hand away. "Of course it matters. I never said it didn't matter, just that it isn't the *only* thing that matters."

"Someone has to take over for me someday," Stuart went on doggedly. "Ben has a degree in business administration."

Ben smiled and nodded.

"And yet he's managing a grain silo in a tiny town in Oklahoma," Rex pointed out. "No offense, Ben."

"None taken," Ben said affably. "At my age, I figure it's better to be a big cog in a small machine than a small cog in a big—"

At Stuart's pointed glare, he broke off and swigged more coffee.

"The point is," Stuart stated flatly, "I have to plan for the future, and if my only flesh and blood is going to throw back in my face my every attempt to protect and provide for her, then I have to look elsewhere."

Callie rolled her eyes. At the same time, Rex said, "Just to be clear, you're talking about disowning your daughter and granddaughter."

"It's not what I'd prefer," Stuart said mournfully. "All I've ever wanted was to take care of my little girl, but I can't fight her forever, and like I said, I have to plan for the future. There are businesses, jobs, the loans that underwrite, all manner of livelihoods at stake here. I need to leave things with someone who I know can handle them."

He shifted; then, so did Ben. Callie got the distinct impression that the first event occasioned the second. When Ben spoke, she was sure of it.

"You know," Ben said, reaching toward Callie, "this doesn't mean all is lost."

"Oh?" She knew instantly what was coming next. She knew, too, that Ben thought he was holding a winning hand at last. In many ways, she felt sorry for him. He must feel as if he'd won the lottery, that he'd fallen into the best deal imaginable, but she knew better. For one thing, she knew her father. For another, she knew herself.

Ben smiled. He really was a nice, if clueless, soul. "If you marry me, you can have it all," he said through a broad smile.

Rex straightened and put his foot back as if he meant to shove his chair away from the table. Callie quickly moved her foot to intercept his. Then she shifted Bodie onto her lap and reached out to cover Ben's hand with her own.

"Ben," she said gently. "I'll be glad to call you brother. But I will *never* call you husband."

"Ohhhh." Ben fell back in his chair, obviously deflated.

Rex parked his elbows on the edge of the table and dropped his face into his hands. Callie had the feeling that he was hiding a smile. Stuart, on the other hand, exploded. He leaped up out of his chair, throwing his arms about wildly. Bodie jerked, surprised by the sudden movement.

"Big words, little girl! But stop for one minute and think what you're giving up!"

Callie shook her head, holding Bodie close. "Maybe you need to stop and think, Dad," she said sternly. "Did you really believe this would work? I gave up everything once before to marry the man of my choice. What makes you think I'd marry the man of *your* choice now just to keep it?"

"Didn't you learn anything married to that church mouse?" Stuart demanded.

"Yes," Callie said, holding Bodie close and looking up at her father. "I learned what it means to be loved and appreciated, that faith and living in God's will is more important than anything else and that I can do anything I must as long as I put my faith in the Lord and seek His will. I also learned," she went on more softly, "how much pain you must have felt when Mom died. I'm sorry for that, Dad. I'm so sorry. But I won't marry a man I don't love just so I won't be hurt when he dies." She glanced at Ben, murmuring, "Sorry, Ben. I like you, but…"

"Aw, that's okay," he said good-naturedly. "I never could see it anyhow."

All the fight seemed to go out of Stuart. He dropped down into his chair again, muttering, "You're both stupid as bricks."

From the other room, Wes called, "What'd he say?"

"Nothing he meant," Rex answered loudly.

Stuart rested his forearms on the edge of the table and beseeched Callie. "I've never known what to do for you. Why can't you see that I cannot just turn over everything to you? You don't have a clue how to manage it all. At least Ben has a chance to keep it going after I'm gone."

"It's not my fault I don't know anything about your businesses," Callie told him. "Since the day I started dating, you've never let me do more than fill in here and there for one of your employees."

"It's a man's job to protect and care for his womenfolk," Stuart retorted.

"I agree with you," Rex put in. "On the other hand, my sister manages one of the major hotels in Dallas, part of a multimillion-dollar corporation. I don't doubt that Callie could run the Straight Arrow now if she had to and still keep the house, which is more than I can do."

Callie looked at him in surprise. "What makes you say that?"

"Oh, come on. I'm not saying you could practice law, but don't try to make me believe you haven't picked up the planting and harvest schedule, the herd inspection routine, the market figures… I know you can balance the books and repair a baler. Maybe you can't ride herd or care for the horses, but that's what the hands are for, and you'd learn. It might be a struggle for a while, but you'd get a handle on it."

"I couldn't do as good a job as you're doing," she told him.

"With the right instruction you could," he refuted. He looked to Stuart then and said, "What makes you think she can't manage your business concerns?"

Stuart started ticking off the businesses on his fingers. "Grocery store, café, gas station, Feed and Grain, silo, majority ownership in the bank, various real estate holdings."

"Can Ben manage all that?" Rex demanded.

"Not yet," Stuart admitted, "but I'm working with him."

"Work with Callie," Rex proposed. "I assume you've got managers."

"More or less. Ben handles the Feed and Grain and the silo. I concentrate on the bank and real estate. Others handle the day-to-day operations at the grocery, café and station."

"I know nothing about banking or real estate," Callie admitted. "The retail end of things is easier."

"Hiring the right help is the key," Rex said. "It seems to me that what Callie has to learn to manage are the managers. Maybe Ben could take a bigger hand in things. We could draw up a reasonable, executable business plan and start educating Callie about how to run it. With Ben and others to help her, I have no doubt that she can learn to handle it. That being the case, she'll never have to depend on *any* man for her financial security."

Stuart stared at Callie as if seeing her for the first time. "Is that something you'd consider?" he asked carefully.

"Much of it is beyond me right now," she admitted, "but if you're willing to teach me, I'm willing to learn." She looked down at Bodie, adding, "I have my own daughter to consider, after all."

"Does that mean you'll come home?" Stuart asked hopefully.

"Not as long as Wes needs me," Callie said, "but eventually, yes. I won't work for nothing, though, Dad. I'll gladly fill in wherever I'm needed and learn whatever is necessary, but I expect to be paid like anyone else."

He nodded slowly. "That's fair."

Callie sneaked a smile to Rex. Then she looked to Ben. "Is all this okay with you, Ben?"

He seemed surprised that she'd asked. "Oh, hey. I've got a good job, and so long as I keep it, I'm happy."

"You don't mind not being adopted?" Rex asked.

"Well, it's not like I'm an orphan," Ben said. "I didn't know how I was going to explain it to my folks, to tell you the truth."

Callie bent her head, hiding her smile.

"So, we're good here now?" Rex asked.

"I'd feel better if she was going home with me," Stuart groused.

"Oh, shut up and get out of here," said Wes good-naturedly, hobbling into the room. "You got what you want and now you're just interfering with my afternoon nap."

Stuart half turned on his chair and hung his arm over the back to glare at Wes, but the glare softened when he saw the condition the other man was in. Wes's clothes hung on his thin frame and his bald head and sparse eyebrows made him look gaunt. Stuart did him the kindness of not letting on how shocked he was, though.

Huffing, Stuart grumbled, "Cancer doesn't give you the right to be rude."

"No? Well, then, there's absolutely no benefit in it." Wes carried his coffee cup to the counter and set it down next to the coffeepot, saying to Callie, "Suppose I could have another slice of that bread?"

"Sure." She got up to go after his plate. She started to hand Bodie to Rex, but then she thought better of it. Walking around the table, she plopped her daughter onto her father's lap and walked out of the room.

"Hiii," Bodie said, looking up at her grandfather.

Callie heard the surprise in her father's voice when he asked, "Is she talking?"

"Sort of," Rex answered. "We doubt she understands what she's saying, but she's starting to imitate sounds. She can say 'Mama' now."

"Mama," Bodie repeated obligingly. The she suddenly called at the top of her lungs, "Ma-ma!"

"Coming," Callie said, picking up the plate from Wes's bedside table and heading back toward the kitchen.

"She knows that word for sure," Stuart said with a chuckle.

"Ma-ma," Bodie said again the instant Callie entered the room.

"Yes, she does know what she's saying," Stuart exclaimed, bouncing her on his knee.

"She's a smart one, that's for sure," Rex said proudly.

Suddenly Bodie twisted and threw herself backward in an effort to reach him. Stuart squawked and latched on to her. At the same time, Rex caught her.

"Hey, kiddo. You're going to crack your skull with that trick one of these days."

"Callie used to do that," Stuart revealed, letting go of her. "Scared me to death."

"I survived, Dad," Callie said, coming to stand at his shoulder. "She will, too."

Stuart patted Callie's back. "Guess you're right," he said.

It was the sweetest moment she'd had with her father in a very long time. She looked to Wes, who kept his distance, leaning against the counter by the coffeepot, and smiled.

"Believe I'll go back to bed," Wes said on a sigh.

"Let me help you," Callie offered, leaving her father's side to offer Wes her arm. "I'll bring your snack after you're settled. We've got to fatten you up."

"If anyone can, you can, Callie girl," Wes told her as she walked him back toward his room. "Stu, good to see you."

"Take care of yourself, Wes," Stuart said.

"That's what I got her for," Wes returned, winking at Callie.

Behind her, she heard Rex say, "Tell you what, Stuart, you figure out what day and time works best for you, and the four of us—me, you, Callie and Ben—will sit down and get started on that business plan."

"Sounds good," Stuart said. "Might be best if we work here, though. I can see that Wes doesn't need to be on his own too long."

"I appreciate that," Rex told him.

"Well," Stuart rumbled, "man's a friend of mine."

"He says the same of you," Rex said.

Callie pressed her cheek to Wes's, whispering, "Thank you."

He patted her hand and pointed a finger skyward. Nodding, Callie closed her eyes and repeated the sentiment.

Thank You. Thank You. Thank You. Thank You.

Chapter Fourteen

"Go start the car, Ben, and cool it off, why don't you?" Stuart directed, handing over the keys. Nodding, Ben hurried off to do as told.

Rex had learned over the last week and more that Ben Dolent—while socially inept, and somewhat lacking in what might be termed *common sense*—was book smart and well organized, with a good head for numbers. What he lacked in looks and personality, he made up for with an utter lack of ill intent. Rex could see why Stuart had decided he would do as a son-in-law, if one overlooked the fact that he was completely unsuited to a strong, bright, intelligent, beautiful woman like Callie. Pairing the two of them would be like pairing a donkey and a thoroughbred.

Stuart turned to Rex and offered his hand. "I think we've made good headway."

Rex shook hands with the older man. "I agree."

"You know, we've never discussed payment for your services," Stuart said, glancing around the porch.

"Oh, you don't owe me anything." Rex looked down at his boots, his thumbs hooked in the waistband of his jeans. "I'm an attorney by trade, not a business planner. Besides, having Callie here is payment enough."

"You won't have her here for long," Stuart remarked gleefully.

Rex couldn't be happy about that. He was prepared to argue that even with Meredith arriving soon, they still needed Callie at Straight Arrow Ranch, but with Ann not far behind, that wouldn't buy him much time. He'd been wondering lately what he'd done.

Suddenly, thanks to him and his bright ideas, Callie Crowsen Deviner was a bona fide heiress, at least by War Bonnet standards. With this newfound peace between her and her father, she didn't need a husband, but that wouldn't keep the single men around town from going after her. Surely even Stuart had to realize this fact.

"You do know that half the county is going to be lining up to entice Callie away from you, don't you?"

Stuart made a face. "A father's nightmare," he grumbled. "I've known it since she was fourteen years old." He scraped Rex with a measuring look, adding, "Frankly, I figured you'd be in the hunt."

"Oh, I'll be at the head of the line," Rex admitted blithely, expecting thunder or perhaps even a fist aimed in his direction. He'd almost welcome either, anything to upset the trajectory they seemed to be on.

To his surprise, Stuart huffed and stepped down off the porch, saying, "Well, I guess she could do worse. You at least know she'll be in complete control of her own inheritance."

That sounded suspiciously like a blessing to Rex, who quipped, "I'll have to charge for prenup agreements. Unless they're my own."

Stuart just snorted and walked off into the night, leaving Rex to wonder in astonishment if the lady would be as amenable to his suit as her father seemed to be. As if summoned by thoughts of her, she pushed through the screen door at his back and stepped out onto the porch with him.

"Oh, it's beautiful out here."

"If you don't mind hot and sticky," Rex said, putting his back to the nearest post.

Callie smiled, wandering closer. "It's so peaceful, though, and the night sky is amazing."

Rex canted his head to look up through the tree branches overhead. "It really is. You forget in the city just how many stars the night sky holds. The ambient light hides them."

"That's sad."

"It is. Neon dazzles, but it just isn't the same."

She turned that lovely green gaze on him then. "I hope that means you're really going to stay."

He couldn't stop his frown. "I keep telling you that I am." Why wouldn't she believe him?

She nodded and turned away, remarking, "You know what this porch needs? A good old-fashioned swing."

"We used to have one," Rex told her. "It broke after Mom died, and Dad never replaced it." An idea struck him, a way to have her to himself for a while. "I think it's time we do that. I have to drive into Ardmore to see a car dealer. Why don't you come with me and help me pick out a porch swing?"

She turned, her own frown in place. "What about Wes?"

"He's seemed stronger lately, don't you think? I'll get Mrs. Lightner to sit with him and Bodie for a few hours."

"Him *and* Bodie?"

"Yeah," Rex said casually. "I have to take my car. It only has two seats."

"Oh. Uh. But how will you get the swing home?"

"Not a problem," he said with a wave of his hand. "Trust me. Got that part all figured out. I just…" He shrugged. "Well, I've never bought a porch swing. Mom's had cushions and this little wicker table next to it for drinks and things. I thought Dad might like to sit out here sometimes." He let that hang in the air for a moment or two. "I could just use some help choosing it all."

She spread her hands. "After everything you've done for me," she began.

"Everything *I've* done for *you*?"

"Hiring me when no one else would, backing down my father at every turn," she went on, "even at great expense to yourself. Finding a way to finally make peace between Dad and me. These weeks here at the ranch have been…" She shook her head as if the words escaped her. "Thank you. Especially for your confidence in me and what you said to my dad when he brought up that adoption nonsense."

"He wasn't serious about that," Rex said with a wrinkle of his nose. "It was just his way of getting his foot in the door." He tried not to be *too* happy about her praise, and then she went and ruined it for him entirely.

"But you—and Wes—you saw what neither my dad nor I did. You've ironed out a lifelong problem, and I know it's going to be better for us from here on out. I'm actually excited about working with him. I can't thank you enough."

Rex shook his head, wishing he didn't feel as if he'd lost her already. "I'd say you're welcome, but everything I've done has been self-serving, Callie. We couldn't have made it without you here. I hope you know that."

She shrugged. Then she fluffed her bangs in that nervous way she had and said, "I could use a cold drink. How does lemonade sound? I think I'll make some lemonade."

"Sounds good," Rex told her, disappointed that she seemed to be looking for a reason to get away from him.

Smiling, she turned and went into the house, saying, "I'll take some to Wes."

Of course she would. She'd do everything she could to help while she was here. And then she'd leave him. Them. Unless he found some way to make her want to stay.

Mrs. Lightner couldn't come the next day, so Rex had to wait until Friday. It was just as well. They would only be gone a few hours, but Callie insisted on cooking as if they'd be gone for days, making sure that meals were prepared ahead of time. Only when she opened the freezer to show Mrs. Lightner where she'd stored the baby's milk did Rex realize that she'd been storing up weeks' worth of prepared meals for when she left the Straight Arrow behind. The sight of all those neatly labeled and stacked containers sent Rex's heart into a panicked gallop.

He practically dragged her outside to the waiting car, which he'd uncovered earlier.

"Wow," she said, looking at the expensive, low-slung Porsche in which he'd taken such pride. "Are you going to put the top down?"

"Sure," he said, holding her elbow as she slid down into the bucket seat. "Since it's the last time I'm ever going to drive it, I intend to enjoy the full experience."

"The last time?" she echoed as he closed her door.

He walked around and dropped down behind the steering wheel before answering her. "Yep."

He'd left his hat behind, but he slid his sunglasses into place before he started the engine. The throaty rumble made him smile. He did like a fast car. Funny, he hadn't thought much about this one in weeks.

"Please tell me you're not selling this to cover paying off the church loan."

He chuckled as he backed the car around and shifted into first. "Nope. I'm trading it for a new truck."

She gaped at him.

"What? It's a really nice truck. Double cab, leather seats, state-of-the-art sound system, all the bells and whistles. Tax deductible, too. You'll like it."

She laughed. "You're really serious. You're staying."

"I keep telling you." He eased the car up onto the dry, red-clay dirt road, reminding himself that it needed oiling before winter. "Hang on," he warned. Then he gunned the engine, popped the clutch and let that bad boy scream. It threw up a red cloud that would be visible for miles.

They were both laughing when they reached the pavement. He stopped long enough to let the cloud settle before he stowed the top. Then he turned east toward Ardmore and tried to keep the speed limit within sight. About halfway there, he offered to let Callie drive, but she declined.

"I'm doing just fine where I am, thank you."

"Okay. It's not that you can't drive a standard, though. Right?"

"Bite your tongue."

He grinned. "Because that's all right. The truck's an automatic, by the way."

"I can drive a standard. Any standard."

"This one's specially geared, but I know you could get the hang of it."

"I'm not driving your car, Rex."

"How about my truck?"

"We'll see."

She drove them to lunch some three hours later in his brand-new ruby-red platinum edition Ford F-450. Every salesman, mechanic and detailer on the lot had come out to see Rex's Porsche when they'd arrived. Rex figured they'd double the mileage on it joyriding in the thing before they got it sold, if they even tried to sell it. From the way the owner of the dealership dickered over the price, Rex assumed that he would be enjoying the car himself. Made no difference to Rex. The way Callie mooned over the truck he'd ordered was enough for him to let the Porsche go without the least regret.

They wound up at an even trade, which was really in the dealership's favor as the heavily customized Boxster Spyder was the most expensive two-seater that Porsche made, but Rex couldn't have been happier to sit up there in the shotgun seat of the pickup truck while Callie drove them off the lot. All through lunch she rhapsodized about the truck.

"I can't believe that little car got you that great big, tricked-out truck. Remind me to take you with me if I ever buy a new car."

Rex smiled. "I'll do that."

"You know your dad's still going to want to ride around with the windows down," she told him, and he laughed.

"Yeah, you're probably right."

"I could just move in," she said. "Seriously. I've lived in worse. Much worse."

"No bathroom," he pointed out, about to say that she could just stay right where she was.

"Really?" she quipped. "It's got everything else."

The waitress showed up just then to see if their meal was satisfactory. Callie asked for mustard for her onion rings.

"You eat mustard on your onion rings?" Rex asked, surprised by this fact he hadn't known about her.

She nodded. "I've always heard that cooked onion and mustard are both good for stomach issues, so I eat them together. By the way, your father's dietician told me not to give him raw onions. I'm sure Meri knows, but I thought I ought to tell you."

That reminder that Meredith would soon arrive and Callie soon go dampened the mood.

"I don't want you to leave us," he said quietly.

For a long moment she sat in silence. Then she said, "It's best for everyone."

Rex wanted to howl and throw things. Instead, he picked up his hamburger and stuffed it into his mouth.

They left the restaurant fifteen minutes later, and Rex drove them to the local office supply store, where he bought a nice combination printer. Then they were off to the home improvement store, where Callie quickly picked out a porch swing and all the necessary accessories. Rex paid for and loaded all the necessary supplies and accessories into the back of his brand-new truck before opening the passenger door for Callie.

Once more he held her by the elbow until she was settled. This time she climbed up rather than down. During the whole process, he fought the almost overwhelming urge to pull her into his arms and kiss her until she figured out everything he couldn't seem to find the words to say. But they were in a public parking lot in broad daylight on a weekday, and he had no confidence that she would welcome his overtures any more than she'd welcomed Ben Dolent's. At least she had to know Rex wasn't after her for her money. Didn't she?

He brooded on that all the way home, and then he walked in the door to find his father sitting at the kitchen table, sipping a cup of coffee, a smile on his face.

"You should see Rex's new truck," Callie said, speaking her first words in almost an hour.

"Can't wait," Wes enthused, getting to his feet, a process noticeably less laborious than only a few days ago.

"Where's Mrs. Lightner?" Callie asked.

"She went up to be sure the phone didn't wake Bodie."

"Who called?" Rex asked, waiting for his dad to reach him so he could walk him out to see the truck.

"Meri." Wes's smile widened. "Her leave has come through at long last. She'll be here on Monday."

Monday. Meredith would arrive on Monday. And Callie would leave.

The world seemed to shift beneath Rex's feet. Giving no sign that she had even heard, Callie went to the counter and began to put away the lunch dishes that Mrs. Lightner had hand-washed and left drying beside the kitchen sink. Wes laid a hand on Rex's arm, recalling him to the moment.

Turning woodenly, Rex walked his father from the room, down the hall and out the back door, where he gave an energetic rundown of the truck's many features, the words spilling out of his mouth without conscious thought, while his heart silently broke.

Callie wanted to cry. She'd known it was coming, and she knew it was for the best, but leaving Straight Arrow Ranch would be one of the most difficult things she'd ever done. Nevertheless, after putting it off as long as she could, she quietly began to pack after dinner on Saturday evening.

It had taken only minutes to throw her things into a few bags and boxes when she'd left her father's house to come here, but she couldn't bring herself to leave the Straight Arrow the same way. Leaving her father's home had been an act of desperation; parting from the Straight Arrow could be done only with gratitude and regret.

She started by carefully folding and packing the winter clothing that she and Bodie hadn't had the chance to wear since coming here. As she did this, her heart bleeding a little more with every garment that she folded and stowed, she listened to the faint sounds of her daughter giggling below stairs as Rex entertained her. He'd learned exactly what tickled Bodie most and would often have the baby howling with laughter that shook her little belly and made her eyes dance with delight. Bodie was going to miss him so much, almost as much as her mother would.

Callie dashed tears from her eyes, boxed some toys and blankets that were rarely used and put it all away for now. She just couldn't face more at the moment. Sitting down in the rocking chair, she stared out the window into the gloomy dusk and tried to pray, thanking God once again for working out her issues with her father. Even as she rejoiced in this new peace with her dad, a pall of silence seemed to settle over the house. She couldn't shake the feeling that this had become a house of mourning.

Rattled, she began to pray for Wes's healing. He would be headed back to Oklahoma City for another chemotherapy treatment before long. But she wouldn't be there this time. She wouldn't be needed, Callie knew. Still, it hurt to think that she wouldn't be an active part of Wes's battle any longer, not there, not here.

She wondered how Rex would manage with the rye and barley that was about ready to harvest. No doubt he would simply put it off for a few days, risking rain, or perhaps he would stay here at the Straight Arrow while Meri accompanied their father to the city for his treatment. If the latter should be the case, then Rex would be here alone. Callie wondered if she could find a way to come out and at least warm up his dinner for him. Maybe her father would give her a car to drive.

She certainly couldn't stay here alone with Rex. She knew it, and Rex had to know it, too.

Once again, she understood that leaving was for the best. Should she stay, Rex would feel that he had to go to the city with his dad if only to avoid being alone here with her. No, with Meredith here, staying made zero sense. She had to face it.

The time to go had arrived.

Callie turned to find Rex standing in the doorway of her bedroom, Bodie in his arms.

"I think we need a dry diaper."

"I can take care of that," Callie said, injecting a brightness she didn't feel into her voice. She rose and went to get her daughter.

Even Bodie seemed oddly subdued as she slipped into her mother's arms. She lay quietly on the foot of Callie's bed, her gaze switching back and forth between her mom and Rex as Callie swiftly changed her. The air seemed charged with unspoken words and unrecognized emotion, so heavy that breathing felt difficult. Callie tried to think of what to say.

I want to stay, but unless you love me, there's just no reason for it.

That would be the same as begging Rex to love her, and if he hadn't come to that on his own, what good was it?

To cover her wavering, Callie decided to go ahead and dress Bodie for bed.

"Will you hold her while I get out her pajamas?"

"Sure."

She passed the baby back to Rex and went to the dresser, trying not to remember how he'd bobbled Bodie in the beginning and compare that with how easily and naturally he handled her now. Like a father. Like a proud, doting father.

We doubt she understands what she's saying, but she's starting to imitate sounds. She can say 'Mama' now... She's a smart one, that's for sure.

We. As if they were a couple raising their daughter together. Callie shook off the thought and concentrated on the task at hand.

The drawer with Bodie's things seemed sadly empty now that her winter clothing had been packed. Callie plucked out the one-piece garment she wanted and took back her daughter, stripping off her little short set and trading it for the soft, knit pajamas.

"Now, you just need feeding, and you'll be all ready for bed."

Rising, she parked Bodie on her hip and moved to the door, but instead of shifting out of her way, Rex lifted both arms and blocked her, bracing his forearms against the doorjamb. Callie had avoided looking him in the eye thus far, but now she tilted back her head and did so.

"Rex?" she queried softly.

"No," he said, with a slight shake of his head. "I can't let you leave."

His blue gaze plumbed hers, speeding her heart and freezing the air in her lungs. She stepped back, not daring to assume, to hope—only to pray.

Chapter Fifteen

He had been unbearably stupid, not to mention cowardly. Rex had been telling himself that after Callie moved back to her father's house he would see her around town, that they would date and he would win her heart that way, but he'd been kidding himself. Deep down, he knew that if he let her out of this house he'd never get her back again. After all, he couldn't be the only man to see what an absolute treasure she was. Ben Dolent wouldn't win her heart but someone would.

It might as well be him. It *had* to be him.

"You can't let me leave," she said, "because…"

"Because I can hardly bear to let you out of my sight," he heard himself say. Her eyes widened, and he feared that he'd frightened her. "I—I know that you've had enough controlling men in your life," he hastened to add. "That's not what this is about."

"Okay," she said cautiously, clutching Bodie a little tighter. "What is it about, then?"

Rubbing a hand over his face, he tried to call upon his training, form a lawyerly argument for why he should step into the role of husband and father for Callie and her baby. Sadly, all he could think about in that moment was himself.

His gaze swept over the baby. He'd never expected to become so fond of that kid. His heart smiled every time she lifted her little arms to him, every time she grinned at him or patted his head. How could he let her grow up without him? He couldn't bear the thought of not being there to see her take her first steps and put together her first sentence and all the other firsts awaiting her.

More than that, he wanted to be at Callie's side when Bodie did those things. He wanted to share Callie's laughter and tears, her joy and pain. He needed to be the one to hold her when fear and worry overshadowed her usual good sense and stalwart faith. How could he work all day and drag his tired body home at night without knowing she'd be there to welcome him?

He gulped down his misgivings and began to speak, praying that the right words would come.

"I can't imagine a day without you anymore."

Callie listened to the quavering timbre of his voice and knew it was one he'd never used in a courtroom. This awkward, solemn man who stepped forward and seized her by the upper arms as if he would make her hear him had never stood before the bar or pleaded a less reasoned, more heartfelt case.

"I don't want anyone else to help me off with my boots when I'm too tired to stand," he said urgently, "o-or flick me with a dishtowel when I tease her."

"I—I'm not sure what you're saying," Callie told him, confused.

As if he fought the urge to shake her, his hands tightened convulsively on her arms. "Who am I going to push in that new porch swing if you leave?" he pleaded. "Who do I sit with in church?"

"Your sisters—"

"My sisters can't replace you," he insisted, "not for me. I love them, but that's not the same."

Callie blinked, wanting to believe he meant

what she hoped he meant. "I—I guess I need more than what you've said so far, Rex."

He cupped one of his big hands against her cheek and the other around Bodie's little head. "How am I supposed to get through the day without seeing these faces or hearing your voices?"

Callie smiled and leaned her cheek into his palm. "We won't abandon you. We'll always be around somewhere."

"That's not good enough!" he exclaimed, dropping his hands to park them at his hips. "What good is saving the ranch if there's nobody to save it for?"

"You were never saving the Straight Arrow for me and Bodie," Callie pointed out.

"But I could be," he said, seizing her and pulling them to him. "You're practically family now. It wouldn't take much to make you both family."

"No?" she asked hopefully.

His gaze swept over her face. "You'd just have to marry me," he said swiftly. "Then you'd have as much right to the Broken Arrow as I do."

Her heart slamming against her ribs, she stared into his agonized blue gaze and softly said, "I love this ranch and everyone on it, but that's not what would keep me here."

"Then what?" Rex demanded, folding her close. "Tell me how I can keep you with me."

Callie took a deep breath and a brave step forward. "Do you love me, Rex?"

He almost melted. The planes and lines of his face relaxed. The arms about her warmed.

"I didn't know I could love anyone as much as I love you."

Tears filled her eyes even as laughter bubbled up inside of her. She went up on tiptoe, wrapping her one free arm around him and hooking her chin over his shoulder as he hugged her.

"I love you, too," she whispered. He hugged her so tightly that her heels lifted off the floor. "You scared me at first because you're so strong and determined," she admitted, "but your heart's so pure that I just couldn't help myself."

He shook his head, straightening to look down at her even as he locked his arm about her waist. "That's you, sweetheart. You're my heart. You make me want to be better than I am, and that's the truth of it."

Callie laid her head on his chest, and Bodie copied her, making them both chuckle. "I've seen your soft side too often to believe that," Callie told him.

Yes, he was strong, far stronger than her father, precisely because of the softness of his heart. He was strong enough to stand up to Stuart whenever necessary and soft enough to love without reservation. He was absolutely everything she could ask for in a man. He was, in fact, well on his way to being every bit the man that Wes was and even more.

"I feel so stupid," Rex muttered, wrapping his arms around Callie and Bodie and leaning back against the doorjamb, "for thinking I was in love before."

Tilting her head back, Callie smiled. "You don't have to say that."

"No, it's true, and I feel bad about it. What Amy and I had was nothing like what my parents had together, and I always knew it. I can't believe I settled for so little. I took so much for granted, made some incredibly foolish choices."

"My father thought that I settled for too little when I married Bo," Callie said carefully.

"But you didn't," Rex stated calmly. "I understand that, Callie, and I'm glad for it. I'm sorry that he died. I don't know why that had to happen, and as happy as I am to have found you, I'm sorry for it."

Callie nodded. "Me, too. But I've realized something recently. So long as Bo lived, I would never have had peace with my father.

Dad could never have understood my choice of such a man as a husband or our way of life. The funny thing is, from the day we married, Bo prayed for my father and me to find that peace. So, in a way, you're the answer to Bo's prayer."

Rex lifted his eyebrows, pulling in a deep breath. "I'll try to remember that whenever Stuart makes me want to smack him."

Chuckling, Callie said, "I suspect that will be often."

"Someday," Rex mused, smoothing a hand over Bodie's head, "I expect to shake Bo Deviner's hand in Heaven."

"I think he'll welcome that."

"I hope so." He nodded at Bodie, adding, "I have much to thank him for."

"So do I," Callie whispered, rubbing her cheek against his chest. "So do I."

"It's strange how God works," Rex mused. "If my dad hadn't gotten ill, I'd never have come back here. I wouldn't have found you. I wouldn't understand that everything I want, all I need is right here. I want my dad to live. I want him to enjoy his grandchildren. I want him to know that this ranch will mean something to future Billings generations. And at the same time, I thank God for whatever it took to bring me here to this moment."

"I understand completely," Callie told him. "Given all you've said, though, maybe we shouldn't wait."

He looked down at her. "You mean it? You'll marry me? Right away?"

She nodded, smiling. "The sooner the better."

He swooped down for a kiss that went on so long Bodie started pulling his hair. "Ow," he said, finally lifting his head. "You are getting your own room again, young lady."

Callie chortled. "You should be prepared for some blowback from my father."

"Somehow," Rex told her, smiling smugly, "I don't think it'll be as bad you might suspect."

Callie lifted her brows at that, but as he was kissing her again, she abandoned the thought. And every other.

Epilogue

The pastor lifted both hands as Rex and Callie turned, beaming, to face the packed sanctuary. "Ladies and gentlemen, I present to you, Mr. and Mrs. Rex Billings." Applause followed. "Callie and Rex, go in peace, with the blessing of God—Father, Son and Holy Spirit. Amen."

The bride, wearing a simple, ankle-length dress of sea green lace and carrying a hand-picked bouquet of peonies, irises and sunflowers, clutched her husband's arm and stepped down off the platform at the front of the church. Rex, in highly polished boots, his best black suit, white shirt and a silk tie the exact color of his wife's dress, stepped down with her, smiling so widely that Wes expected his face to crack at any moment. Wes's own face ached from all the smiling he'd done in the past four days. Now if only he could see his daughters as happily settled before he left this world…

At least Ann had shown up for her brother's wedding with a fiancé in tow, though the two hardly seemed as starry-eyed as Rex and Callie. Wes wondered if the pair would have waited even four days if Ann could have gotten here any sooner. The hasty wedding suited Wes just fine. Time, after all, was not a luxury for him these days.

He watched from his wheelchair as Meredith, who had served as Callie's maid of honor, took Stuart Crowsen's arm and stepped down off the platform to follow the bride and groom. She looked lovely in a dress a shade darker green than the bride. The color complemented her strawberry blond hair.

Asking Stuart to act as best man had been a stroke of genius on Rex's part. Stu had blustered and barked when confronted with his daughter's plan to marry, but anyone who knew Stu could have seen that his temper fit had been all for show. Stu Crowsen was no one's fool. He was delighted to have Rex for a son-in-law.

"Let's go, Dad," Ann said, taking his hand while her fiancé and coworker, Jordan Teel, grasped the handles of the chair, pushing it forward. Tall and sophisticated in her pale suit, her muted red hair twisted into a sleek chignon on the back of her head, Ann caught many an appreciative eye.

Wes wished that he had more in common with Jordan. The handsome, urbane hotelier seemed a little old for Ann and somewhat uncomfortable in his current surroundings. He'd had to go to Ardmore to find a room, which he'd let everyone know was far, far below his usual standards. Nevertheless, if Ann was happy with Jordan Teel, Wes would try to be happy for her, just as he'd tried to be happy for Rex when he'd married Amy Gladden.

Teel seemed like a nice enough man. No one could deny that he was intelligent and successful, and the diamond that he'd parked on Ann's finger was the size of an auto and likely cost more. He and Ann looked like the perfect couple. Meredith seemed thrilled for her sister. Rex appeared accepting, but he was so fixated on Callie that Wes could discount his judgment at the moment.

The bride had baked her own wedding cake, and it awaited the guests back at the Straight Arrow. The happy couple took their daughter from Mrs. Lightner, tucked her into her car seat in the back of the cab of Rex's new truck then climbed in the front for the ride to the ranch. Dean Pryor, the custom cutter they'd hired to harvest the oats and late sorghum, and the ranch hands Duffy, Cam and Woody, and Cam's teenage son, Luther, had tied strings of cans onto the back of the expensive truck and decorated it with "Just Married" graffiti. That truck, Wes knew, was the envy of many a cowboy around War Bonnet, so they'd been especially careful with it, not that Rex seemed to mind. Right now all he cared about was that Callie was his.

Meri and Wes had ridden in Stu's Cadillac. Jordan pushed Wes's wheelchair over to the luxury auto and held it steady while Wes got to his feet. He really didn't need the chair, but his children had insisted, and he hadn't wanted to cause any turmoil. Wes let himself into the front passenger seat while Jordan folded the chair and stowed it in the trunk.

Already behind the wheel, Stu muttered, "He better treat her right."

Wes chuckled. "He'll treat her better than you did. He loves her, Stu. He loves her like you loved Jane, like I loved Glory. Can't ask for more than that."

"No," Stu admitted quietly. "Can't ask for more than that."

Meredith got into the backseat, the door opened for her by Dean Pryor. "Thanks, Dean. See you at the ranch."

"Wouldn't miss it," Dean said, a hand on the shoulder of his young son. Donovan's white blond hair hung in his eyes, but his snaggle-toothed grin proclaimed him a happy boy.

He, Stuart and Meredith made the drive back to the ranch house. They arrived at the ranch to find Dr. Alice Shorter and the veterinarian, Stark Burns, crouched in the middle of the dirt road in front of the old red barn. Wes felt the bottom drop out of his stomach.

"My cat!" Meredith cried out, opening her car door even before Stuart brought the vehicle to a safe halt. She was out and running in her strappy heels before Wes could even caution her.

He saw Stark rise and turn, a bloody towel and its contents cradled in his arms. At the same time, Alice hurried forward to intercept Meredith.

"Oh, no," Wes said, closing his eyes. "Please, God, don't let that cat be dead," he prayed. They didn't need a tragedy, however minor, on a wedding day.

Stark carried his burden to his pickup truck and climbed up inside, ignoring Meredith's pleas to go with him.

"There's no time," Wes heard Alice say as he hurried toward his daughter. "And you should be here with your brother."

"Don't you let my cat die!" Meredith yelled at Stark as he began maneuvering the truck, one-handed, out of the line of vehicles parked alongside the dirt road.

"He'll do everything he can," Wes assured her, sliding his arm across Meredith's shoulders and turning her toward the house. He looked to Alice over the top of her head but was not reassured by the worried expression in the doctor's eyes or the slight shake of her head.

Callie and Rex met them on the porch. Rex carried Bodie, outfitted in a delicate pink dress, in the curve of his arm.

"I'm so sorry," Callie said to Meredith. "One of the church ladies preparing the reception opened your bedroom door while looking for the upstairs bathroom and the cat got out."

"It's my fault," Meredith told her morosely. "I should've put both cats in their carriers before I went to the church." She hurried off to confine the second cat before it, too, met with an accident.

"At least Dr. Burns was here when the cat got run over," Callie said with a sympathetic grimace.

"True. Except she'll never forgive him if that thing dies," Rex muttered.

"Now, don't worry," Stuart instructed,

brushing past her to get to the front door. "This is your wedding day."

Callie leaned against Rex, smiling. "I can't believe how many people showed up. I hope we have enough food."

Wes chuckled. "Daughter, we'll be fine. You've cooked enough for armies."

"You need to get off your feet and away from the crowd," Alice reminded him.

"Not until I've welcomed our guests and Stuart and I have prayed a blessing on this marriage," Wes told her firmly. She rolled her eyes, ever the doubter, but he didn't believe she doubted nearly as much as she pretended.

He offered her his arm, and she gave him a long look before taking it. She was a fine-looking woman, Alice Shorter, but stubborn, unbelievably stubborn. Wes smiled to himself. He could think of worst traits in a woman.

They followed Rex and Callie into the house. The old place felt bursting with new life. He expected plenty of changes in the days ahead, and that was fine by him. Life was change, and this change felt right.

Rex and Callie would leave in a few hours for a secret destination, returning on Saturday to pick up Bodie before taking a week to empty Rex's condo in Tulsa and put it up for sale. That didn't seem like much of a wedding trip to Wes, but they insisted that was how they wanted to do things. Rex had some fine leather furniture he intended to use here, and he meant to make some renovations to the house with the funds from the sale of the condo.

Meanwhile, Meredith and Ann would have a couple days to get to know their new niece, and Ann would stay on to oversee the custom cutting while Meredith escorted Wes back to Oklahoma City for his second chemotherapy treatment. Then Ann would return to Dallas until her company sent a temporary replacement for her—or she changed her mind about coming home.

With Rex moving home permanently and Callie now part of the family, Ann didn't have to pitch in quite as much as they'd first figured. Besides, Wes couldn't shake the feeling that Jordan would prefer that she stay in Dallas.

Looking around at the crowd of family and friends that surrounded him, his son, new daughter-in-law and granddaughter at his side, his daughters smiling broadly, his dining table about to collapse beneath the bounty arrayed atop it, Wes nodded to his old friend. Stuart lifted his hands in a signal for quiet.

"Will you join the father of the groom and me for prayer?"

Heads bowed as Stuart began to pray.

"Oh, Lord, You have joined two families as one today…"

Wes smiled. Yes, change had come to Straight Arrow Ranch. No one could know how it would all end, but so be it. Wes hoped that he would still be here to see it all play out, not that it truly mattered. If he had learned anything in his sixty-three years, it was that God knows best.

Looking at his happy son's beaming face, Wes took great comfort in that one eternal truth.

God always knows best.

* * * * *

If you loved this story, pick up these other stories of small-town life from author Arlene James's previous miniseries:

*CHATAM HOUSE
THE DOCTOR'S PERFECT MATCH
THE BACHELOR MEETS HIS MATCH
HIS IDEAL MATCH
BUILDING A PERFECT MATCH.*

Available now from Love Inspired!

*Find more great reads at
www.LoveInspired.com*

Dear Reader,

Going home can be tough, especially when you've told everyone, including yourself, it's the last place you want to be. On the other hand, despite the difficulty, going home can turn out to be an overwhelming blessing when it is where you truly belong and where God wants you.

The prodigal son of Scripture learned that lesson the hard way. God often allows difficulty to drive us in the direction we should go, but when we react in humble obedience, He rewards us with unexpected blessings.

Rex Billings thought ranch life was too hard and sought an easier path to success, only to find that labor is labor, whether physical or mental, and that a combination of the two brought him the greatest satisfaction imaginable. Like so many of us, he couldn't see the forest because of the trees—until someone helped him adjust his focus.

May your focus always be true.

God bless,

Arlene James

REQUEST YOUR FREE BOOKS!
2 FREE WHOLESOME ROMANCE NOVELS IN LARGER PRINT
PLUS 2
FREE
MYSTERY GIFTS

⁂ ⁂

HEARTWARMING™

⁂ ⁂

Wholesome, tender romances

YES! Please send me 2 FREE Harlequin® Heartwarming Larger-Print novels and my 2 FREE mystery gifts (gifts worth about $10). After receiving them, if I don't wish to receive any more books, I can return the shipping statement marked "cancel." If I don't cancel, I will receive 4 brand-new larger-print novels every month and be billed just $5.24 per book in the U.S. or $5.99 per book in Canada. That's a savings of at least 19% off the cover price. It's quite a bargain! Shipping and handling is just 50¢ per book in the U.S. and 75¢ per book in Canada.* I understand that accepting the 2 free books and gifts places me under no obligation to buy anything. I can always return a shipment and cancel at any time. Even if I never buy another book, the two free books and gifts are mine to keep forever.

161/361 IDN GHX2

Name _____ (PLEASE PRINT)

Address _____ Apt. #

City _____ State/Prov. _____ Zip/Postal Code

Signature (if under 18, a parent or guardian must sign)

Mail to the **Reader Service:**
IN U.S.A.: P.O. Box 1867, Buffalo, NY 14240-1867
IN CANADA: P.O. Box 609, Fort Erie, Ontario L2A 5X3

* Terms and prices subject to change without notice. Prices do not include applicable taxes. Sales tax applicable in N.Y. Canadian residents will be charged applicable taxes. Offer not valid in Quebec. This offer is limited to one order per household. Not valid for current subscribers to Harlequin Heartwarming larger-print books. All orders subject to credit approval. Credit or debit balances in a customer's account(s) may be offset by any other outstanding balance owed by or to the customer. Please allow 4 to 6 weeks for delivery. Offer available while quantities last.

Your Privacy—The Reader Service is committed to protecting your privacy. Our Privacy Policy is available online at www.ReaderService.com or upon request from the Reader Service.

We make a portion of our mailing list available to reputable third parties that offer products we believe may interest you. If you prefer that we not exchange your name with third parties, or if you wish to clarify or modify your communication preferences, please visit us at www.ReaderService.com/consumerchoice or write to us at Reader Service Preference Service, P.O. Box 9062, Buffalo, NY 14240-9062. Include your complete name and address.

HWI5

WESTERN (WP) PROMISES

YES! Please send me **The Western Promises Collection** in Larger Print. This collection begins with 3 FREE books and 2 FREE gifts (gifts valued at approx. $14.00 retail) in the first shipment, along with the other first 4 books from the collection! If I do not cancel, I will receive 8 monthly shipments until I have the entire 51-book Western Promises collection. I will receive 2 or 3 FREE books in each shipment and I will pay just $4.99 US/ $5.89 CDN for each of the other four books in each shipment, plus $2.99 for shipping and handling per shipment. *If I decide to keep the entire collection, I'll have paid for only 32 books, because 19 books are FREE! I understand that accepting the 3 free books and gifts places me under no obligation to buy anything. I can always return a shipment and cancel at any time. My free books and gifts are mine to keep no matter what I decide.

272 HCN 3070 472 HCN 3070

Name	(PLEASE PRINT)

Address	Apt. #

City	State/Prov.	Zip/Postal Code

Signature (if under 18, a parent or guardian must sign)

Mail to the **Reader Service**:
IN U.S.A.: P.O. Box 1867, Buffalo, NY 14240-1867
IN CANADA: P.O. Box 609, Fort Erie, Ontario L2A 5X3

* Terms and prices subject to change without notice. Prices do not include applicable taxes. Sales tax applicable in N.Y. Canadian residents will be charged applicable taxes. This offer is limited to one order per household. All orders subject to approval. Credit or debit balances in a customer's account(s) may be offset by any other outstanding balance owed by or to the customer. Please allow 4 to 6 weeks for delivery. Offer available while quantities last. Offer not available to Quebec residents.

Your Privacy—The Reader Service is committed to protecting your privacy. Our Privacy Policy is available online at www.ReaderService.com or upon request from the Reader Service.

We make a portion of our mailing list available to reputable third parties that offer products we believe may interest you. If you prefer that we not exchange your name with third parties, or if you wish to clarify or modify your communication preferences, please visit us at www.ReaderService.com/consumerschoice or write to us at Reader Service Preference Service, P.O. Box 9062, Buffalo, NY 14240-9062. Include your complete name and address.